KING ARTHUR
—— AND THE ——
KNIGHTS OF THE ROUND
TABLE

KING ARTHUR
——— AND THE ———
KNIGHTS OF THE
ROUND TABLE

Retold by Phyllis Briggs

Abridged edition

DEAN

This edition published 1992 by Dean,
part of Reed International Books Ltd.,
Michelin House, 81 Fulham Road, London SW3 6RB

This edition first published 1957 by Dean & Son Ltd.

ISBN 0 603 55073 8

Printed and bound in Italy by OFSA S.p.A.

CONTENTS

CONTENTS

8

CHAPTER I

HOW THE KING WAS CHOSEN

IN THE great days of chivalry in England, long, long years ago, a child was born to King Uther Pendragon and Queen Igraine. Those times were very hard, fierce and unsettled, with bickerings between the knights and wars between the kings.

The King's wise counsellor, Merlin, came to him in the great tapestried chamber where he sat. The cold east wind sifted in through the unglazed windows and harried the flames up the stone chimney, so that smoke puffed out into the room.

"This court is no place in which to bring up your son," Merlin said. "Let some brave knight of yours take him and teach him, as befits a man, all the noble deeds of arms that he must do!"

"But whom can I trust?" said the King.

"Sir Ector, lord of wide lands in England and in Wales, shall take him—he is faithful and true!"

"As you will," said King Uther, and he sighed, for he knew in his secret heart that he himself would never live to see his boy, Arthur, mount his first horse or splinter his first lance.

So through the echoing passages they carried the baby boy, all dressed in cloth-of-gold, to the postern gate of the castle. There Sir Ector was waiting as he had been told to do, and he took charge of the small bundle.

During the next two years the unrest in the kingdom grew worse, and King Uther was a sick man and could not hold the people together. Battles broke out, great castles were besieged and taken, and men died by sword and lance.

King Uther fought his last battle on the grassy fields at St. Albans and won a last victory over his enemies. But after a triumphal entry into the frowning city of London, he lay down to die, heedless of the cheering people and fluttering banners.

"The King must name his son, Arthur, to reign after him," Merlin warned the great barons. "I will call you all together tomorrow that you may hear him speak!"

The King lay white and still, but as the great men crowded round him, he raised himself and cried: "I give him God's blessing and mine own, and I say he shall claim the throne when he has grown to man's estate, and he shall rule after me."

The uneasy years passed, and little Arthur grew to manhood on the far-off estates of good Sir Ector. He never dreamed how evil men were all quarrelling as to who should be king of the fair land, and he knew nothing of his own high birth.

Wise old Merlin held his peace until he thought it was time to act; then he went to the Archbishop of Canterbury, for he knew that the people must have a sign to tell them who should reign over them in a way that would bring them peace and happiness.

"Call all men to London to pray for a great miracle that shall show us our way," Merlin advised.

The Archbishop nodded his old, white head, and he called for parchment and pen. The summons went out to all nobles, gentlemen-at-arms, barons and knights, that they should come to London and pray in the great church. Soon, through country lanes and on the great highways, were the twinkle of arms and the rustle of leather trappings, as the long lines of men wended south-east. From the marches of Wales and the flat salt-flats of East Anglia, from the blood-soaked borders of Scotland and from the great estates of the west, came the knights to London.

In the cold dark before dawn on a Christmas morning they went into the church to pray, while their squires led their proud horses away through the snow to the stables. There was stamping and clanking, torches flashed and men shouted, but in the church the candles winked peacefully on the rows of silent, praying knights.

Then someone cried in terror that there had appeared in the churchyard a marble stone with a steel anvil upon it, and in the anvil was stuck a naked sword with gold letters shining upon the hilt.

The frightened, breathless people shivered as a learned clerk read out the words.

"Whoso pulleth out this sword from this stone and anvil is rightful king of all England."

When the service was over and all the men had come out of the church they stood around to marvel at the miracle, and some of them tried to draw the sword, thinking that they would be king. But not one of them could stir it.

"He is not yet come," the Archbishop said. "We will set knights to guard the sword meanwhile. Stay here in London, all men, and joust and make a tournament so that you keep together, and let any man who likes try to draw the sword!"

Christmas passed and New Year came and still no one had been found who could stir that blade from the stone.

Riding to the tournament came Sir Ector with his own son, Sir Kay, and the young man, Arthur.

"Brother, I have lost my sword," said Sir Kay. "Mayhap I left it at our lodgings. Will you ride back and bring it to me?"

"I will well," Arthur answered, with his sunny smile, and he turned his horse and rode back. But the place was deserted, for all the people were at the jousting. "Sir Kay shall not be without a sword this day," Arthur mused. "I will ride on into the churchyard and take the sword that is in the stone!"

But there was no one there, either; the tent of the guarding knights was empty and the stone deserted, for the men had gone to the tournament. No one saw the handsome young man as he rode up, tall and strong and confident, the light of kingship shining in his eyes. His armour was plain, his surcoat un-blazoned, his head bare. He swung down from his saddle and tied up his horse and then he went forward and grasped the mighty handle of the sword. Frost twinkled on the steel; the sun blazed upon the golden letters as if in warning that only the rightful king might essay this great deed; but lightly and confidently Arthur drew out the sword and rode away with it and gave it to Sir Kay.

Sir Kay recognised it and was troubled in his mind. To his father he said: "Sir, does this thing mean that I am king of England?"

The old knight frowned in doubt upon his boy. Before his glance even the bravest had quailed, for he was a hard, just man, to whom the rules of chivalry were as binding as his own honour.

"We will test this," he said, and he took the two boys with him back into the dark church, and there he made Sir Kay lay his hand upon the great hand-written Bible.

"Now, tell me how you got the sword," he said.

"My brother Arthur brought it to me," Sir Kay answered simply.

The old man wheeled upon his adopted son. "And how did you come by it?"

"I pulled it from the stone," Arthur replied.

"Then you are king of all this land," Sir Ector said in wonder and awe.

The young man was startled and dismayed. "Why, and for what cause?" he cried.

"For God will have it so," Sir Ector answered. "Now let us see if you can put it there as it was and pull it out again!"

"That needs no skill," Arthur cried, and he raised his arm and stabbed the great sword back again into the stone, where it stuck quivering as before.

Sir Ector tried to pull it out, but he could not, and then Sir Kay tried, and he could not.

"Now shall you essay it," said the old knight to Arthur.

"I will do it," said Arthur, and he drew the sword.

Sir Ector and Sir Kay kneeled down before him.

"Alas and alas!" said the young man. "My loved father and brother, why are you kneeling to me?"

"Nay," answered the old man. "You were never son of mine nor of my blood." And, kneeling there, he told him all the story.

Arthur was greatly distressed to learn that Sir Ector was not his true father.

"But promise me you will be a good king and rule well over us," said the old knight.

"How could I do else?" Arthur answered. "For I owe you most of all. I will always love you and your good wife, who has been a mother to me. I will make my foster-brother, your son, seneschal of all my lands, if it is as you say and I am king!"

They told the Archbishop that the great deed had been done, and so, on the twelfth day after Christmas, the barons met and there before them all young Arthur pulled out the great sword.

Some of the powerful lords who had tried in vain to do it were furiously jealous and began to stir up trouble, saying that it was a shame a mere boy should be set over them. So the whole decision was put off till Candlemas. Ten good knights yet watched over the sword day and night. At Candlemas the knights and nobles tried their strength again, but as it was at Christmas, so it was then. No man could draw the sword save only Arthur.

But still they grumbled and put the whole thing off till Easter. The spring winds came and the snow melted away and daisies starred the grass and the feast of Easter came. All men tried to essay the sword of kingship, but none could prevail. Then Arthur drew the sword and flashed the blade aloft, but though some men would have him for king, yet many nobles could not believe that this stripling should rule, and they put the matter off till Pentecost, thinking that by then some great champion would have arisen. A small body of faithful knights was set about Arthur to be his bodyguard and serve him, and one of these knights was Sir Kay.

At Pentecost, Arthur drew the sword again in the sight of all the nobles and the common men, and these last crowded to him and shouted that they would have him for their king.

"We see it is God's will," they cried, "and any who will not obey us and do this thing we will slay!"

All that great crowd, rich and poor, kneeled down before him, the nobles in silk and velvet and ermine, the poor men in homespun and galligaskins, the knights and squires in their armour—some new and bright, some rusty and battle-worn. They asked for mercy because they had so doubted. Arthur forgave them, and then he took the sword and marched into the great church. Bowing his head reverently, he laid the sword on the altar.

The best and truest man there then made Arthur a knight, and he was crowned in grim old London as many many kings and princes were yet to be crowned through the coming years of history. His subjects came to do him honour and brought complaints for him to hear and wrongs to right. He gave back to their owners lands that had been stolen from them. His rule began wisely and well.

Sir Kay he made seneschal as he had promised, and Sir Baudwin he made constable, and Sir Brastias he made warden. And after a few years he had won over to his rule all the North and Scotland and Wales and all the fair rolling lands of England.

CHAPTER 2

HOW THE KING GOT HIS SWORD

INTO the courtyard of King Arthur's castle a young man rode one summer evening. He led another horse, on which sat a man all huddled together, his armour broken, his surcoat stained and torn. His squire was in an agony of grief.

"My master is wounded and dying," he told the King. "A knight has set up his pavilion by the fountain in the forest and he will let no one by unless he fights him. Will no one go and stop this thing and avenge my poor master?"

"Make me a knight," whispered one young squire to the King. "I will take this deed on myself!"

King Arthur hesitated. "Thou art very young for knighthood," he said seriously, and old Merlin, who was hard by, plucked at the King's sleeve.

"He is indeed too young," he growled. "This knight in the forest must be a mighty fighter, and if you lose this young man, Griflet, you lose a future brave supporter of your throne."

"Do not refuse me," Griflet begged. "I have served you faithfully, and this matter of knighthood is a thing that no man shall do for me but you only."

King Arthur stood musing by the window and listening to the clamour in the yard below, where all the knights were lamenting the dead knight and giving their advice.

"I will do it," he said suddenly. "Bring me my sword and I will make you a belted knight. Arise, Sir Griflet. Now that I have given you your wish you must give me a promise!"

"Anything," answered the new knight eagerly.

"Then promise that, after jousting with this bold knight at the fountain, you will come straight back to me without taking on further adventure."

"I promise!" cried the young man, and he hastened off to get his horse and his armour.

He took a long ash spear and rode off with his heart high with the excitement of adventure. By the fountain was a tent, and near it a fine horse stood already saddled. Hung on a tree was the challenging knight's shield, so Sir Griflet struck it with his spear and sent it rolling among the bracken. A big, bronzed man strode out of the tent, his armour clanking as he moved.

"Fair sir, why did you that?" he asked stonily, his cold eyes on the young knight.

"I will break a lance with you," said Sir Griflet.

"You had better not; you are but a youth," said the other.

"Still will I break a lance with you," said Sir Griflet.

The big man could not well hold back any more, but he seemed uneasy.

"Where are you from?" he asked, as he mounted his beautiful horse.

"From the court of King Arthur," Sir Griflet replied proudly.

Without more talk the two knights urged their horses forward through the quiet of the summer glade. Their spears splintered with the force of the meeting, but Sir Griflet was no match for the older man and he and his horse went crashing down in a heap. The big knight unlaced his helm so that he could breathe freely.

"You are a brave lad," he said, "and if you live you will be a famous knight. Now, get you gone!"

Painfully and slowly, Sir Griflet rode back to the court, where there was a great outcry at sight of him. His wounds were dressed, but he lay many weary days recovering from the encounter. King Arthur was grieved for him, and he made up his mind that he would take on the business himself, though he was no older than Sir Griflet and not yet so hardy nor so clever a fighter as the knight by the fountain.

As he rode towards the place he met old Merlin, his counsellor, who followed him, much troubled about the matter.

"Do you go to your death?" Merlin asked warningly. "This is a very strong man, who will have no more pity on your youth than he had on Sir Griflet's."

"So he must be stopped," said King Arthur, "for he makes our forest ways dangerous."

"Sir knight," he said when he came to the pavilion, "why will you let no one pass?"

"It is a custom of mine," replied the other.

"Then had you better give up the custom," Arthur stated, but the stranger knight shrugged.

"If any man disagrees with me, let him stop me," he said.

"That I will an' gladly," answered the King, and set his lance in rest.

Both combatants' spears were shattered as they rode together, but they fought on with swords, on foot, and old Merlin stood under the trees, stroking his beard and shaking his head. Through the peaceful, golden afternoon the two fought, but so well matched were they that neither seemed to prevail. Though he was younger and lighter, yet King Arthur's courage was so high, his eye so quick, and his foot so nimble, that stroke for stroke he matched the stranger knight. Then suddenly his sword broke in his hand and he was left defenceless.

"You must yield you now," cried the knight, whose name was Sir Pellinore. "Confess yourself as recreant or I will slay you!"

"Slay me an' you must," the King gasped, "but recreant no man shall ever call me. And I still can fight, as you shall see."

He leaped forward, threw his arms about the knight's waist, and carried him to the ground with the shock of the surprise. Over and over they rolled, striving for mastery, and the frightened red squirrels ran scolding away. But here weight told heavily against King Arthur. Sir Pellinore drew his dagger to make a finish, and there would have been a sad end to the King if Merlin had not interposed and by a secret art made a deep sleep overpower Sir Pellinore.

"You have killed him," King Arthur accused angrily. "He was a fine knight and I would rather have lost a kingdom than cause him to lie helpless there!"

"He is safe," Merlin assured him. "In three hours he will awake. I warned you what you were attempting. There is not a better man nor finer fighter in all this wide realm than he, and he shall be of good service to you in the long years to come. Now, come you with me to a hermit I know and he shall heal your hurts and make you whole again. In three days, perchance, you may ride again."

"But, alas, I have now no sword," sighed the King.

"You shall have such a sword as no knight has ever had yet," Merlin told him softly.

When King Arthur was well again they rode away together. On the way they passed a broad lake on which floated fair lilies. In the centre was a very strange sight, for there was an arm raised above the dimpled water, and it held a sword.

"There is your weapon," Merlin said, "and look yonder at that maiden—for she is the Lady of the Lake. Speak her fair and ask her for the gift of the sword."

There was something passing strange and almost frightening about the figure as it glided up to them, but King Arthur showed no fear, however fast beat his heart.

"Maiden," the King said, "I would that sword were mine, for I have none."

She nodded slowly, and told him that for his bravery he should have it, and if she ever wanted a favour in return, why then she would seek it at the right time.

There was an old barge among the reeds, so Arthur and Merlin stepped into it and rowed across the lake. The King gripped the wonderful sword and at once the hand let go its grasp and slipped away under the water, leaving a silver trail of bubbles.

"It is a noble sword," cried the King as they rode away. His eyes were shining, for here truly was a blade with which to seek adventure and high honour.

"Which like you best, sword or scabbard?" Merlin asked.

"The sword—in truth, I like the sword best," Arthur said, his cheeks flushing with pleasure, for it was a blade such as no man had ever seen.

"Hot youth," Merlin muttered. "You are not as wise as you think. The scabbard is worth far more than many such swords, for while you wear it no drop of blood shall you lose. Now ride we back to your castle in Carlion, for you have been a long time away."

All King Arthur's knights rejoiced when they saw him. Some of the older ones shook their heads at his risking his life in such a manner, but they all agreed that it was meet to be ruled by a king who did not fear to endanger his own life for adventure.

CHAPTER 3

THE COMING OF THE TABLE ROUND

IN THE hot days of August when the common men were out in the fields about Camelot—which is now our city of Winchester —cutting their crops of barley and herding the swine, King Arthur sent for Merlin to seek his advice.

"My barons give me no peace," Arthur said. "They all say that the kingdom should have a fair queen and so I needs must wed!"

Merlin nodded. "They are quite right, noble sire. Is there any great lady whom you love more than another?"

The King nodded. "I am not worthy—she is so lovely—but I love Guinevere, daughter of King Leodegrance. He is that king who has in his house a strange table—the Table Round. You said that it belonged once to my father, King Uther, and that he gave it to him."

"That is true," Merlin made reply. "Now, as to this matter of the wedding. Will you grant to me the task of fetching your bride to meet you in London?"

Eagerly King Arthur gave permission, and Merlin got ready, for it was quite a journey to the land of Cameliard, which was where Guinevere's father ruled. He was received with pomp into the old grey castle; meats were baked, and wine was poured. After he had rested and eaten, Merlin was asked by King Leodegrance for his message from King Arthur. When he heard of the honour being done to his house, he smiled.

"This is proud news," he said, "that the great and worthy King Arthur should wish to marry Guinevere!"

"Nay, the honour is done to King Arthur," said Merlin, who was very wise and knew how to get his way. "But will so lovely a damosel smile upon him?"

"My daughter does as I tell her," said King Leodegrance shortly. "She will wed King Arthur. Now, as to the dowry— shall I give Arthur a gift of lands who has more land now than he knows well what to do with? I know"—and he clapped his hands together so that the goblets on the banqueting table chinked together—"I will give him the Table Round that old Uther Pendragon gave to me many a long year agone. One hundred and fifty knights can sit about it at one time and there is not such a wondrous table in all England. Five-score of my own bold knights shall go with it. There has been much fighting of late and I have lost brave and hardy men. King Arthur must make up the tally himself!"

"That will he do right gladly," Merlin said. "Now, an ye will prepare a litter for the lady, we will start for London by sunrise!"

That was a right royal progress across England, and many a peasant stood and gaped and scratched his head and marvelled at it. They journeyed by barge where they could, and by land where they had to, and so, slowly, they wended their way to the capital. Two knights, noted for their furious riding, went on ahead with the news, and a bustle of preparation began in the strong, walled city on the Thames. Bells rang, and flowers and branches of green trees were torn down to decorate the houses. Documents about the wedding and the Queen's coronation were written out by clerks and monks and sealed with the King's great seal.

Happy that he was to marry the lady he loved so truly, King Arthur set to work to complete all the matters that needed attention. To Merlin he gave the task of looking round and choosing fifty of the bravest, best, and worthiest knights in the kingdom to fill up the empty places at the Round Table. The King was determined that in future days it should become a hallmark of true goodness and worth to be called a Knight of the Round Table. None should be granted the privilege but proven men. The task was none too easy. There were many brave and bold knights, it is true, but they were not always *good*. Sometimes they were greedy or cruel or careless and King Arthur would have none of them.

"I can find only twenty-eight true men," Merlin told the King.

So the beautifully carved seats about the table, called in those days sieges, would not all be filled.

"No matter," King Arthur said; "time will fill them. Now sit ye down in your sieges that I may see how it likes me!"

It was a fine sight in that old raftered hall, with the sunlight streaming through the coloured glass of the windows, to see the one hundred and twenty-eight knights taking their places. Their swords and armour shone and winked and their embroidered surcoats rustled.

"Now we will all go and do homage to the King," Merlin commanded. "Arise, fair sirs, and follow me. I thank you for your courtesy. The King will be very pleased with his Knights of the Table Round!"

And then a very strange thing came to pass, for where each knight had been set at table there was his name in letters of gold upon the back of his siege.

"I would like much to be a Knight of the Round Table," mused Gawaine, who was the King's nephew. "But, alack, they will say I am too young for the honour, though in very sooth my heart burns for deeds of high renown, and I can ride and break a lance with any who will joust with me!"

He was afraid to speak about it and then remembered that even if a man should feel fear—and what man does not at times?— he must still do that which is his duty or be deemed recreant and false. So he squared his shoulders and set his chin, and went to King Arthur.

"A boon, sir," he begged.

"What do you ask?" the King asked, smiling kindly on the good-looking boy before him.

"Make me a knight on your wedding-day," Gawaine managed to plead.

The King liked bravery and he smiled. "I will do that right gladly," he said. "We must fill the empty places at the Round Table with worthy knights."

"Here there is another suppliant," said a herald. "But I doubt, sire, that he is worthy to come here. He is muddy and smells of the cowhouse!"

Arthur frowned. "A knight's first duty is to treat all men as brothers," he said sternly, and the abashed herald backed away.

Into the hall tottered an old, feeble man clad in shabby homespun, and with old rags tied round his bony legs and feet. His hair was thin and tangled, but his eyes were bright. With him was a young man.

"Great and noble King," the old fellow began, "they do tell me that you will grant any wish of any of your subjects at this happy time if within reason."

"That is right," King Arthur answered kindly. "I did indeed cause my heralds to proclaim this."

"Graciously said, sire! Then I do ask you to make my son here a knight!"

"This is a weighty matter," King Arthur said gravely. "First, what is your name?"

"Aries, the cowherd."

"Is this your wish or his?" the King asked curiously, looking at the young man whose fair and open face seemed to stamp him as of finer blood than a peasant's.

"Nay, it is all his wish," Aries answered hastily. "I have thirteen other boys and they have no such notions. They will do what I say: Clean the sties, or milk, or cut the crops, but I cannot get a day's work out of this one, who spends his time shooting and is at every jousting."

"Your name, boy?" Arthur asked.

"Sire, it is Tor."

King Arthur wondered the more he looked at him, for he was a goodly youth, tall and clean-limbed and very strong. A thought came to him. "Send for your other sons, Aries," he suggested. "I would see them also!"

"I will well," answered the cowherd, and he sent word to his home that the lads were to drop everything and hie them to the King's castle without an instant's delay.

When they trooped into the hall they all looked exactly like copies of the old man, but more youthful. King Arthur mused and smiled.

"Where is the sword, Aries, that is to be used to knight the boy?" he asked.

"Here, sire," said Tor eagerly, and proffered a well-cared-for but old-fashioned sword, which was evidently his treasure.

"Draw it and give it to me, my boy, and ask your boon yourself, as befits a brave man."

Trembling with eagerness, Tor stepped forward and kneeled down, holding the hilt of the drawn sword towards his King. His golden head was proudly held, his blue eyes shone with noble purpose.

"Sire, if you will, I pray that you will allow me to enter the high order of chivalry!"

"Certes," said King Arthur; "it is not for me to hold any man back from high emprise!" He touched Tor lightly on the shoulder. "Be a great and valiant knight, Sir Tor. I will pray to God that you shall be so, for there are many places to fill at the Round Table. Now tell us, O far-sighted and cunning advisor, tell us all, Merlin: shall Sir Tor carry himself worshipfully and become a good knight?"

"Kings' blood runs in his veins," replied Merlin, "for understand, sire, that this worthy Aries, the cowherd, is not his father. The lad is son to King Pellinore, but the old man and his good wife did not know this, having had the care of him since he was born, and being simple folk had forgotten that he was not their own."

King Arthur smiled on the old cowherd. "Ye have lost a useless hand among the cows and I have gained me a fine knight," he said. "Now must we have King Pellinore with us too. The sieges are being filled one by one. It is good."

CHAPTER 4

THE ADVENTURE OF SIR GAWAINE

IN THE church of St. Stephen's in Camelot, that year, King Arthur wedded Dame Guinevere. All the people rejoiced, for the Queen was sweet, and very fair to look upon, and in her robes she looked indeed a very queen!

The common men as well as the barons were pleased and King Arthur was right joyful. Then after came the great feast, and all the worthy knights sat at the Round Table, each in his place, while boars' heads and spiced ale, pasties and rich meats, were carried in. Overhead, fluttering in the draughts, were the King's banner and the knights' pennants, all blazoned with gold and azure and gules.

Two places were yet empty at the table and no golden letters had appeared upon them, so none knew to whom they might belong.

King Arthur turned to Merlin. "For whom are those two sieges?" he asked. "It is a passing strange thing that they should be empty."

Merlin shook his head slowly. "Ah, sire, there shall no man sit in either of those sieges but he that is most worthy in all Christendom. This siege"—and he laid his hand reverently upon the carved back of one of them—"this is the Siege Perilous, and in this place no man but one shall ever sit and live. He who dares this thing, and, unworthy in his heart, holds any slighting thought or evil intent shall be destroyed! The man who sits here must have no peer in any land, in any time. Years of the future shall come upon us and roll away till far-off times of which we can guess nothing, but never again shall there breathe a man such as the one who shall sit here and grace your court!"

"These are very curious words," said Arthur. "But we will await events and see what adventures shall be achieved in this manner."

"As to that, sire," Merlin replied, "let your knights hold themselves in readiness, for at this moment there comes a venture to try some of them."

As he spoke, there was a clamour without, and into the hall leaped a white hart, sore-pressed and panting, and after it a white hound and thirty couples of black hounds. Round the table went the hunt and so away again, but before it was out of sight men said that a knight had captured the white hound and borne it off. Some said that a lady on a white palfrey had cried aloud that the hound was hers, and that another knight had carried off the lady so that her laments died away in the distance.

"It is well," cried King Arthur, "for it was all a most unseemly noise."

"Not so," Merlin said. "This thing may not rest here, for it were dishonour to your knights not to seek advancement and worship in this matter."

"What do you suggest?" the King asked.

"Three knights shall take up this adventure," Merlin said. "And then they shall return and tell us all that happened, and it shall be a test for them and an example to us all. Sir Gawaine, stand up and let me see thee. It is well! You shall ride your ways and bring again the white hart. Sir Tor, he must ride and bring again the white hound, and King Pellinore, he must ride and rescue the lady who was so shamefully carried off. Arm ye and ride, for ye shall have great honour."

Sir Gawaine was ready first, and with his brother, Gaheris, to act as squire he rode out into the darkling woods which lay about the fair town of Camelot. His heart was high with hope, for this was his first adventure as a knight and all the world seemed to be before him. But, alas, he knew not how hot blood and anger should bring down his vaulting pride. A good knight is better for being humble.

Presently they came to a glade in the wood all trampled and dashed flat by the stamping of two horses on which sat two knights fighting desperately with one another.

Sir Gawaine and his brother rode between to stop them, for so exhausted were the two that they could hardly raise their sword arms longer.

"What are you fighting for? It must be some heavy matter," Sir Gawaine asked.

"We are brothers," one of the men answered. "A white hart passed this way and we were fighting to decide who should follow it, and we have not solved the question yet."

"Nor shall ye with this foolishness," Sir Gawaine answered. "Now hearken to me. You shall go to the court of King Arthur and say you were sent with greetings from the knight who chases the white hart!"

The brothers considered awhile. "It shall be as you say, fair sir," said one; "for indeed we have lost so much blood and are so weak we cannot dispute with you nor fight more."

And so they both rode off and Sir Gawaine continued his quest. He overthrew any who stood in his way, and at long last he and Gaheris reached a castle, to which the white hart ran for shelter. Here they let slip greyhounds, and these chased the hart into the courtyard, pulled it down, and killed it.

"We will carry it back to King Arthur's court and show them all that we achieved what we were sent to do," said Sir Gawaine.

But at that moment, a fierce knight, fully armed, came clashing out into the yard with his sword drawn and his face dark with anger. Straight away he slew two of the hounds and chased the others off.

"That was my white hart, given to me by a fair lady," he thundered. "I will take vengeance on you, sir knight, for this was an evil thing that you did!"

"Rather I would that you took vengeance on me than on my hounds," Sir Gawaine replied. "They knew no better, but did as all hounds do. You should not have slain them!"

Then Sir Gawaine dismounted, for he held it dishonour to have such an advantage over a fighter on foot. They rushed at each other and began to hack and hew so mightily that their armour dented and cracked. Then with one terrific blow Sir Gawaine brought the stranger knight to his knees.

"Do not kill me, as you are a knight and a gentleman," the vanquished man begged. "I pray you, give me my life."

His fair lady came running from the castle, her face alight with fear and streaked with tears, but Gawaine did not see her.

All his hot blood was roused by the fight and he forgot the rules of chivalry and honour. A red mist floated in front of his eyes and he raised his sword to kill the other knight, when he should have spared him. The lady tried in vain to protect her loved knight by throwing herself between them, and, to Sir Gawaine's horror, his blow went home by misadventure and she fell lifeless at his feet.

Sir Gawaine was so shocked that he stood there as if turned to stone. At last, with trembling lips, he whispered: "I will give you your life, sir knight!"

"It is of no use to me now," replied the stricken man. "You have slain that which was more to me than all the world."

"You have shamed your knight's honour," said Gaheris in horrified tones to his brother. "As long as you live you will remember this day and flinch at the thought of what you did."

"It is true," Gawaine muttered, overcome by grief. To the vanquished knight he said: "I shall send you to King Arthur's court, where you will say you were beaten in fair fight by the knight who followed the white hart. But in truth I know not if ever I may return and show my pennant there again."

"I will go," said the knight, and so he departed.

Then came four men out of the castle and fell upon Sir Gawaine and Gaheris and fought so bitterly that they overcame them and took them prisoners and shut them up in the castle, where they sat repenting sadly in the cold and dark, with their bruises and wounds grieving them very sore. And there they were all that night, listening to the rats scuttling and the thud-thud of sentries' feet upon the walls. But in the morning, some of the good ladies of the castle spoke for them and let them go, and they gave Sir Gawaine the head of the white hart, for it had been his quest and he must show it at court as proof that he had accomplished his adventure.

And so the two returned to Camelot in a very different frame of mind from that in which they had ridden out.

King Arthur was greatly displeased when he heard the story, and all the court was shocked that the new-made knight had borne himself so ungently. He had to swear before them all that he would spend the rest of his life helping all women, rich or poor, humble or noble, in remembrance of the fair lady he had so foully slain.

So ended his adventure, and they all waited to hear what Sir Tor had achieved.

CHAPTER 5

THE ADVENTURE OF SIR TOR

SIR TOR had set out quietly upon his venture, with none of the dashing valour of Sir Gawaine. Sir Tor's arms were old and worn, being only such pieces as he had collected with loving care over a year's time.

King Pellinore saw his son patiently fitting the rusty pieces upon himself, and he smiled with pride, for this new-found boy of his was what he felt all followers of chivalry should be: high of purpose but humble of mien.

"The armour is rusty, certainly," King Pellinore said to King Arthur as they stood watching, themselves unseen, "but his eyes are bright as steel. If the shield is outworn, the courage is not. Think you he means to adventure himself just as he is and without horse?"

"That shall not be!" King Arthur cried warmly. "Shame were it on me if I let a knight of mine face his venture thus. Squire, bring hither from the great chest my suit of plate inlaid and the sword with the jewelled hilt. Bring also the plumed helm of Milan work. Sir Tor shall not part from us till he is so fitted out as befits a king's son!"

King Pellinore stroked his beard and his eyes twinkled. "Arthur, Arthur, you leave nothing for me to do for my son," he said. "Nay, there is one thing. Squire, go to the stables and bring here my great war-horse with the trappings of carved leather and silverwork. A knight needs such a horse if he is to win advancement!"

When Sir Tor saw these presents he was much moved and his face shone with joy at so much goodly workmanship. And so he rode from Camelot, alone, to find the white hound. And this was his first adventure.

Slowly he wended his way through the forest land, studying the tracks of the wild things as they wandered up the woody ways, and listening to the songs of the birds. His heart was happy and his smile joyful.

Into his path stepped a dwarf as woefully ugly as he himself was handsome. The dwarf had slunk out of the bushes twirling a staff twice as long as himself. He capered upon the leafy pathway, threatening with his heavy staff and leering evilly, his small dark face twisted with a grimace.

Pity for the misshapen wretch was in Sir Tor's heart, for he felt that it must be a terrible thing to be so short and heavy, with such bandy legs that he could never don armour nor sit a horse as a proper man should.

The dwarf seemed filled with some revengeful spirit of cruelty, for suddenly he sprang forward and struck Sir Tor's charger on the head so that it reared and backed, pawing the air in terror. If he had not been a good horseman, Sir Tor would have fared ill.

"Why did you do that?" he asked quietly, when he had mastered and comforted his steed. "Methinks it was a most ungentle thing to do, seeing that neither I nor this poor brute had harmed you."

The dwarf shook himself and brandished his staff again. "It matters not, sir knight. You may not ride by here unless you first have ado with my brave masters, who wait in yonder pavilions!"

"Are not the forest ways free?" asked Sir Tor mildly. "It is a strange thing that within King Arthur's realm, a bowshot's length from Camelot, a man cannot come and go as he will."

"You may not pass," repeated the dwarf sullenly.

Sir Tor looked at the pavilions and at the shields hung upon the oaks and at the great jousting-spears standing there, their points winking in the sunshine. Regret was in his face as he shook his head.

"Good dwarf, it may not be. I have a quest to ride, one given me at the Round Table, and I must go on and give a good account of myself or else be deemed recreant."

"I will force your decision," said the dwarf.

He seized a hunting horn that swung at his belt and blew a loud summons upon it. The flap of the pavilion was dashed aside and a fully-armed man came out and mounted his waiting beast. He came galloping towards them, dried leaves scattering from his horse's feet. Sir Tor smiled, for now he knew that this was part of his venture and that he might encounter this knight and dispute with him without being false to his mission. He crooked his arm and gripped his lance and spurred his brave horse forward from a trot to a gallop. With a crash the two met, but Sir Tor was the better man, in greater command of himself and his animal. True on its mark his spear struck, and, rocklike, he held in his saddle so that the other man went hurtling to the earth.

"Do you yield yourself?" Sir Tor asked as the fallen knight picked himself up and made to catch his horse.

"Yes, sir stranger knight. You can pass by these ways for me, for hardier nor better stroke I never felt. But I have a fellow knight yonder who also seeks worshipful adventure and I pray you that you will run a course with him also."

"I will welcome him as I did you," Sir Tor answered. "Let him ride out against me."

"He comes now," said the dwarf, who had been standing watching, a puzzled expression in his eyes, as if for the first time a doubt had assailed him as to whether his masters were as glorious champions as he had imagined. The second knight came charging down, the plumes streaming out from his helm. It was a colourful sight to see two such knights as Sir Tor and his adversary under the summer trees.

Their spears splintered with the shock, but again Sir Tor was the victor and the second knight yielded himself and asked for mercy.

"It ill becomes me to kill you who have given me such a pleasant meeting," Sir Tor answered; "but you must both of you do me a service. Go to King Arthur's court and surrender to him."

"When he asks us who sent us what name shall we give?"

"Say simply that you were sent by the knight who rides in

B

the quest of the white hound. And so go in peace and with my blessing, for you be both very worthy men. What names do you bear?"

They told him humbly enough that he had vanquished those knights of high renown, Sir Felot and Sir Petipase. And so they rode away down the forest glades to Camelot.

"If it please you, fair sir," said a voice, and Sir Tor looked down in astonishment, for here was a mighty change. The dwarf's arrogant looks were all gone, his lumpy shoulders were bowed, his eyes beseeched like those of a hunted and beaten dog. "A boon, a boon!" he cried. "Forgive my manners of a while ago, forget my foul blow, and grant me a boon."

"If I can, I will," Sir Tor answered kindly. "If you repent yourself, the matter is already forgotten by me. What is your request, good dwarf?"

"Let me serve you and be your man. Right faithfully will I follow you, for you will not cast me off when I am no more use, as did those recreant knights who rode away with no more thought of where I should sup and bed me than if I had been a dried leaf blown away by the evening wind!"

"Poor misshapen man, your boon is granted. Get you a horse if you may and you shall ride with me, and so forth we will go to adventure and glory!"

Gratefully, the dwarf did as he was told, and so, as the sun was setting like burning gold, they made their way into a thick forest of scented pines, where the gloom was as the night.

"You ride in quest of the white hound?" asked the dwarf. "Then I can help you, for I know where it is. See, through this opening down into yonder valley there stands a pavilion and a hound that bays the moon so that his voice echoes to us even here. There is your white hound, Sir Tor!"

So Sir Tor rode down and took the white hound. The flap of the pavilion was raised and a lady came out.

"Do not touch that hound," she said sternly.

"I must take him," said Sir Tor, "for this is my quest, and from distant Camelot have I ridden to fetch it, and perchance also the knight who bore it off, if I may meet him!"

"You will meet him," said the lady, "and he will make you regret that ever you took on this quest."

"I will abide what fate comes to me," said King Arthur's knight, and he picked up the white hound and set it before him on the saddle and so rode back to the dwarf.

"Do you know of any lodging where we may pass the night?" he asked.

The dwarf looked doubtful. "There is a hermitage within a mile's riding, but I do not know what lodging you will find there."

"So we have shelter for our beasts, it matters not for us," Sir Tor said. "A man should be able to lie hard and go hungry."

After a while they came to the hermitage, and the good old man took them in.

"There is corn for the noble horses," he said smiling, "but dry crusts are all that I have to set before you."

"It matters not," he was answered lightly.

All night long, while the wolves howled in the forest and the winds moaned in the branches of the pines, they slept there. By candlelight, before the dawn, they rose.

"And now we must ride away," Sir Tor said. "Fare you well, good old man, and pray for me that I may carry myself in knightly manner at all times and in all places where I shall be."

All that morning they rode back towards Camelot, but before they reached there they were overtaken by a rider who came shouting after them to give back the white hound.

"It is the knight of which the lady spoke who would do me great mischief if he could," Sir Tor told the dwarf. "Take you the hound and hold it for me and I will meet him."

He laid his lance in rest and turned his horse to face his foe, and so the two charged together. So mighty was the force of their meeting that both were thrown from the saddle. But eagerly they rose and drew their swords and fought bravely, fought on and on till their arms became weary and heavy as lead and they felt weak and faint. At last Sir Tor forced the other man down and he called upon him to yield.

"No, that will I not," was the arrogant answer. "Give me the white hound!"

"I cannot," Sir Tor answered calmly. "It is in my quest, and I must bring it or you or both back with me!"

"Kill him!" cried a voice, and there rode a lady towards them. Her eyes were wild with grief and her face flushed with weeping. "Grant me this boon and kill him, as you are a knight and a gentleman! He is false, a traitor and a murderer—he slew my brother before my eyes!"

"I will grant this boon if it is indeed as you say," Sir Tor cried sternly. He looked down at the fallen knight, who now in terror crept to his feet, his face betraying his guilt.

"Nay, do not kill me, I will yield me," he said in haste. "You can take the white hound!"

Sir Tor's blue eyes were cold as steel. "It is too late now or I shall be false to my promise to this lady. You should have yielded when I asked you. Now you must die for your shameful deed."

The false coward staggered to his feet and tried to make off, but Sir Tor followed and killed him.

"Now shall you and your servant and your poor, tired, hungry horses fare well this day," said the lady. "You shall ride with me to my husband's castle and stay awhile with us. He is full of stories of olden wars and ambushes and we will eat together."

"Thanks for your bounty," said Sir Tor, smiling; "but as for the horses, they fared right well on corn while the men scraped the empty trenchers."

"That shall we amend," laughed the lady, "and whenever you are in these marches our castle and all we own is at your service."

Sir Tor spent a wondrous pleasant evening in the grim old fortalice in the pine-forest. The knight and his lady and Sir Tor and his new squire sat them down to meat together; capons and pasties were set out for them and warm straw for their beasts. All the afternoon and long into the night they sat up singing ballads and telling stories. Sir Tor's eyes shone and he listened with delight to the tales of adventure and daring that the old knight told while his lady sat by the hearth embroidering a banner.

When at last Sir Tor returned to Camelot, he was received with great joy and they made him tell his adventures, though he was ill at ease and shy and did not wish to speak.

"These are but a boy's summer japes compared with the great deeds this king's son shall do," said wise old Merlin. "He shall be one of the best of all your knights, and true and faithful."

"Then must we reward him now," said King Arthur, and he gave him an earldom of lands that was in his gift; "for we must not forget that had King Pellinore and I not espied him in time this boy was about to venture all in an outworn suit of mail and a useless old sword. Truly it is not the arms that make the man!"

CHAPTER 6

THE ADVENTURE OF KING PELLINORE

"Now shall I essay adventure," said King Pellinore, when he prepared to follow and bring back the lady that was stolen from King Arthur's court.

It was this adventure, as you shall hear, that was the chief cause of the drawing up of the special rules of chivalry and knighthood of the Round Table which King Arthur ordered. It seemed to the King that not all men were patient, courteous, and brave, and he was determined that his knights should be so or never call themselves Knights of the Round Table.

As King Pellinore rode along, fully armed, his horse curveting and stepping high, his plumes waving and tossing, his looks proud and confident, he came by a woodland well, and there sat a maiden supporting a wounded knight in her arms. The knight's helm lay shattered by his side, his face was white as the wood-lilies that grew about him, blood was dried upon his lips, and his eyes were closed.

"Help me, fair knight," cried the maiden, wringing her hands. "Help me, King Pellinore, for this good knight I love sorely and I know not how to help him!"

Now King Pellinore looked on the wounded man and he knew that he was doomed. He himself was in haste to proceed with his adventure and he disliked the idea of tarrying to nurse a vanquished knight.

"Help me," the maiden cried again piteously, but King Pellinore drove his spurs into his horse's sides and thundered away from that place. Yet, for all the noise he made, he heard her dolorous cries behind him like the moaning of the wood-doves.

On and on he galloped, till his beast was weary, and at last he drew rein. His heart told him that he had not acted in knightly manner, and already he was sorry for it. But now only the song of the birds at eventide came floating to him and the golden light of the setting sun breathed peace. Coming towards him was a poor labouring man, returning home after toiling all day in the stony fields. He stood in marvelling admiration of the great knight with his blazoned shield and mighty lance.

"Tell me, fellow," said King Pellinore. "Have ye seen a knight pass this way who was carrying off a lady against her will?"

The man pulled at his forelock and gaped anew. "Yes, in sooth, fair sir, they passed this way, and the lady was lamenting. Down there in the woods they have met with a knight who is fighting for her. She is sitting in a tent with the squires, while her fate is decided in battle. Hark ye—over yonder!"

And there, even from that distance, King Pellinore could hear the clash of steel and the neighing of horses.

"This is a noble adventure," he thought and he tried to forget that other maiden by the well whom he had deserted. With pounding of hooves and the clash and creak of harness, King Pellinore rode his horse towards the place, where he went straight to the tent and looked within. The fighting men hard by were too engrossed to notice him. "Lady," said King Pellinore, "come with me to the court of King Arthur again, for I have come to bring you rescue this day."

But the squires shook their heads and said that it could not be unless King Pellinore could part the fighting men and bring them to amity. If he did that the lady would be free to go with him.

"That is good advice," said Pellinore, "for it were a sad thing to go and leave them debating." And he rode down upon the knights, who were now fighting afoot. "Why do you fight so sore?" he asked them when he had ridden between them.

They drew off panting and leaned on their swords; then they told him why. Sir Hontzlake was he who had carried off the lady, and Sir Meliot was he who would rescue her.

"Fight no more," said King Pellinore, "for I have promised King Arthur to bring this lady back safe or die in the attempt. Therefore, if fight you must, then fight with me!" And he swung his horse to ride away down the glade so as to return at the charge, as was the custom.

But Sir Hontzlake raised his sword and stabbed his horse and killed it.

"Fight on foot, as we do!" he said contemptuously. "It were shame to attack us mounted."

"For that I will slay you," said King Pellinore, in a rage at the death of his favourite charger.

In his hot-headed way he did not stop to think that if he had shown fairness from the start it would not have happened thus. So he fought furiously with the knights and with one stroke killed Sir Hontzlake. Then he turned to make an end of Sir Meliot.

But Sir Meliot kneeled down before him. "The lady is my cousin," he said, "and I know that she is safe with you, therefore take her back to the court, as you have rescued her."

"What is this?" cried the other. "Will you not fight for her?"

"What boots it?" said Sir Meliot. "You are a man of great prowess. Put her to no villainy as you are a true knight!"

"That I can promise on my honour," said King Pellinore, and he thought again of the maiden by the well to whom he had behaved so ill.

Taking Sir Hontzlake's horse, he took the bridle of the Lady Nimue's horse and led her away with him. When once more they were come to the forest well, he could not help glancing anxiously at the place where the maiden had sat.

"Alack, and what is this?" cried Nimue, her eyes widening in horror. "Here lies a dead knight and right fair of face he is, and

—oh, woe, woe!—see the sweet maiden dead by her own hand, because, I doubt not, of her grief that her love was slain!".

King Pellinore could not look her in the face, but the tears of bitter remorse gathered in his eyes and he began to weep sore.

"I could have rescued her from this," he groaned. "All this now lies at my door, and she so fair, so very fair, and so young!"

Nimue looked upon him pityingly. "Grieve not on this, sir knight," she advised. "Tears will not help her now. Take up the poor bodies and we will wend to a hermitage and there they shall have burial and peace. That is all you can do now. A chance for knightly adventure have you lost and it will not come again. No man can warm himself by yesterday's sunshine!"

So, still weeping, King Pellinore took up the bodies on his broad shoulders and bore them to the hermit, and he did all as the lady bade him.

At King Arthur's court there was great pleasure when King Pellinore rode into the yard with the Lady Nimue. He must quickly tell all his adventures, said Queen Guinevere, for in sooth she loved to hear tales of prowess. But when King Pellinore had told all, a silence fell upon the court. At last the Queen spoke.

"This is sad hearing, King Pellinore. The blame lies heavily upon you!"

"I repent me deeply," said the knight. "I shall never forget this day, but, as it was, I was so eager about the quest that I could stop for nothing."

Then King Arthur stood up and made a pronouncement to them all, charging them from that day on to flee from treason and lies, to do no murder, to refrain from all wickedness and cruelty, to give mercy to all who begged for it, to hold all womenkind in highest honour, and to fight to the death for them; never to fight in an evil cause nor for gain of money or goods.

"My knights shall be known in all future times as the patterns of chivalry," he cried, and his tones rang down the halls of Camelot. "Pass before me, one by one, and kneel and give me your hands between mine own, and swear each man of you to do my will in this!"

With clashing steps and grave faces, they moved slowly by, and each man swore to obey. And from that time on at each feast of Pentecost was this thing enacted before King Arthur and Queen Guinevere until such times as the King was dead and the times changed and the Round Table knights were all scattered and gone.

CHAPTER 7

THE GREAT BATTLE

IT WAS an early winter's evening at Camelot, and King Arthur was sitting on his great throne holding grave counsel with his allies, the kings and princes of the nearby kingdoms. Day had drained away out of the leaden sky and, with the flush of sunset, had died. So now the fires were piled high and torches smoked and glowed. The gatemen were just raising the drawbridge when a trumpet call announced the coming of ambassadors from Rome.

"Let them be admitted," King Arthur said, and he glanced with deep interest at the twelve men who filed in, waving olive branches as they came.

"I pray thee observe them, Sir Kay," the King said behind his hand; "they are as much like eagles themselves as anything, and it is fitting seeing that they come from the Emperor Lucius. See the hooked, beak-like noses and the bald pates!"

The messengers prostrated themselves before the King, and their leader spoke. But at his words, all pleasantry fled from the face of the company and a stern look of disapproval took its place.

"The Emperor Lucius sends greeting to the King of Britain. He commands that you acknowledge him as overlord and send him fitting tribute in gold."

King Arthur's face darkened. "Commands?" he muttered. "Who is it that commands King Arthur?"

"If," went on the spokesman haughtily, "if this just demand is thrust on one side and set at naught—know then, King Arthur,

that a heavy war shall be waged against you. It will be a war
in which you will go down in red ruin, for you will be treated
as an insolent puppy."

The Knights of the Round Table looked anxiously at King
Arthur, fearing that in his anger he might forget the rules of
hospitality, but they need not have doubted him. Quelling his
temper, King Arthur requested the messengers to withdraw, and
sent one of his greatest knights to show them to a lodging.

Sir Kay and some of the older men drew their swords and
stepped in front of the young knights and squires, who were so
burning with rage at this insult to their loved king and leader
that they would have rushed down the echoing hall and cut down
the old men as they shuffled out.

"Bethink you, it were shame on you," Sir Bedivere shouted.
"What, would you so sully your new-made vows? Sir Uwaine,
strike them with the flat of your blade, so. Cool your ardour
and keep your sword thrusts for knaves, young gerfalcons!"

"It is well," said King Arthur. "Now I pray you, Sir Kay,
see that the Romans have all good cheer and are well entreated
and we will give them an answer in the morning. Gather round
me, good my lords and nobles, and give me your advice!"

They sat long talking and disputing, but the conclusion
reached was always the same: Britain owed no tribute to Rome
and would refuse any.

"And if it is war," said an old warrior, Sir Marhaus, "well,
we may die defending our beliefs, but we will contrive that each
of us shall take a score or so of these braggarts with us. We will
carry this dispute right up to the gates of Rome."

"He smells the conflict already." Arthur smiled. "It is well.
We will answer this messenger of the Emperor Lucius's in
straight terms and take what fate is due to us!"

The King of Scotland rose and spoke. "I will furnish two
thousand men of war," he growled, "and I will lead them for
you when you say the word."

The King of Little Britain jumped to his feet. "And I," he
cried, "I will bring thirty thousand stout men."

With a flutter of silk and ermine, the Lord of West Wales rose
and waved for attention. "Thirty thousand men I too will bring,"

he said and cast a triumphant glance at the King of Little Britain, who merely shrugged.

Sir Uwaine likewise promised to swell the ranks with his son, cousins and as many men-at-arms as he could muster. Then there arose in that hall a knight who had not so very long ago joined the worshipful company of the Knights of the Round Table. He had a fine figure and was darkly handsome, reminding one of a summer storm which backs up, purpling, against the mountains; for high and fierce was the glance of his dark eyes; his slightly waving hair hung to his shoulders and was also softly dark so that the gold circlet upon his brows shone by contrast. Strong were his muscles, so that men could mark the swell and curve of them beneath his purple silk robe.

"It is Sir Launcelot of the Lake," whispered one awestruck young squire at the back of the hall.

"I will bring all my men—and myself too," Sir Launcelot declared. "I would not be away from such a mêlée as this will prove, no, not for all the jewels of the Orient!"

"I thank you all," King Arthur said warmly. "We will give them our answer and bid them depart, and then we will commence such a preparation as has never been matched in all Christendom. At York we will assemble a Parliament and there settle all details; that will be a good centre for all. From Sandwich will we set sail. Let all the ships, galleys, cogges and dromoundes be collected and in readiness with stores of water, biscuits and salted beef!"

Then there began in the rolling green lands of Britain a gathering and a work at which all men marvelled. From Wales to Northumbria, from York to Hastings, the forge-fires were lighted and the armourers set to work. Under their clanging hammers the armour of plate grew from the anvil. Basinets and breastplates, lance-heads and shields—piece by piece they were made and stacked in readiness. Men skilled in such things picked over the seasoning ash and oak poles and cut and polished the great spears. The bowmen went into the fields and set up their targets and they shot from sunrise to star-rise till the meanest of them could shoot a second arrow upon a first and split it from feather to head.

Nor was the work of the women forgotten. In many a cold turret-room and baronial hall the fair ladies sat and sewed banner and pennant with silk and wool and gold thread.

Then came the day of departure. King Arthur appointed two governors to rule the realm for him while he was away.

"And I leave in your care my sweetest flower, my Queen," he said, and for the first time sadness crept into his voice and his heart was heavy.

As he rode away from her, Queen Guinevere's eyes swam with tears. She uttered a loud cry and then swooned, so that her weeping ladies had to carry her to her room.

From the Kentish port sailed the British fleet, rolling and pitching on the blue Channel rollers, so that salt spray dried white upon the gilded sails. Those who had never journeyed so before were terrified, though they strove not to show it, but it was a right fearsome thing to see the sea mouthing at them with foamy lips as if to devour them.

When the coast of Flanders was sighted a great cry went up as the ships headed in for Barflete in that fair land. King Arthur was joined by many more great nobles who were allies of his. And so began the advance upon the army of the Emperor Lucius, who was marching with his men to meet and subdue King Arthur.

On the hills overlooking the vale of Sessoine, the British king drew up his army. To Sir Cador he gave the honourable position of defending the rear. Sir Launcelot, Sir Bors, Sir Kay and others he appointed to be near him and to defend the royal banner.

"Our ladies will expect us to do great deeds this day," King Arthur said. "Hold high your hearts, for when this battle is done, be it for us or against us, it will be the mightiest passage of arms that ever was fought out upon these marches. Many today will do deeds of valour that will be recounted again and again in minstrelsy through years to come, as long as men are brave and hardy and fair ladies love to hear of them! Now, Sir Kay, what think you? Is this a good place we have chosen from which to charge?"

"Meseems it could not be improved," the wise seneschal said.

"An outrider has just come in, sire, to report that the Emperor Lucius is just entering the vale of Sessoine. Nay, hark to that!"

On the cool morning air came the battle-call of trumpets from the advancing army.

"Never heard I such a muster of trumpets," King Arthur said. "The very ground shakes and echoes to them. Our brother knights of Italy seem to need a very hearty summons to fight."

"That is not well," said Sir Launcelot moodily. "What honour and glory is there for us if they be craven knights whose blood must be roused by such a clamour or ever they will draw steel?"

"Not so," said King Arthur. "They will show you of what mettle they are soon and you shall not complain then that you have chicken-hearts to contend with."

"That liketh me well," said Sir Bors.

"Let the army advance," King Arthur cried. "Forward with my royal banner; we will ride to meet them. Who will be first to strike down a foe? After me! Follow your King, and let the battle be to the bravest. Advance, advance!"

Like two waves on golden sands, like two clouds in stormy weather, the armies of Britain and Rome rolled ponderously together. From the heights where the golden eagle nested it appeared as if two seas of coloured light, twisting and tossing, were soaking across the land to blend in such a foam and flurry, such a tumult and clash, as echoed to the farthest hills.

If all the noble deeds and valiant prowess, all the arts and crafts of generalship, all the brave rescues and fierce attacks of that day were written out at length, many and many a volume of vellum sheets would be filled, and many a monk and clerk and scrivener would grow heart-weary with the long task.

Where there was most ado and the mightiest peril, there was King Arthur and his Knights of the Round Table. With Excalibur, his noble sword, in his hand, Arthur drove his destrier wherever the need of blows was most urgent. One second he was fighting with a giant of a man whose weight of attack overbore all who essayed to exchange strokes with him, and hardly had he hewn him down than next moment he was attacked by three knights at once and he must hew and hack, twist and turn as best he might till he had killed or disabled them.

All through the long day raged the fight. One hour it seemed as if the Romans would be victorious, and the next the British host gained ground and drove the other army back, debating every inch of the red-soaked earth.

The sun slanted to a setting and still the clang and din and dolour of the great fight went on. Then King Arthur saw amid a striving mass of fighters the eagle standard of the Emperor Lucius, and he drove his spurs into his horse's sides and urged it towards the place.

"Defend thee, knight," he called to Lucius. "This day shall we settle for all time whether or no I owe you tribute or you owe me service!"

Lucius heard, but he nothing feared, for he was a brave fighter. Like a whirlwind of steel, his blade flashed about his head as he flourished it. Then the two men met. Almost the first blow of the Emperor struck Arthur across the face, shattering his visor and hurting him sore. He knew the wound was serious and he also knew that if he were struck down his followers would lose heart and perhaps be beaten and slaughtered.

"It must not be," he muttered, and he felt his strength mounting. His eyes flashed fire, he swung up Excalibur, and down came such a stroke upon the head of the Emperor Lucius that men tell of it to this day and hold their breath in horror. No metal harness, no arms forged, could withstand that grievous stroke, which cleft his head from crown to chin so that the Emperor fell dead from his charger.

Thus the end of the battle came to pass, for all the heart went out of the Romans when they saw their emperor fall. And men still talk about that fight, the battle of Sessoine, when tens and tens of thousands fell upon the blood-soaked field. The flower of Roman knighthood died that day. The Sultan of Syria was among the dead, also the kings of Egypt and Ethiopia, seventeen other lesser kings and sixty senators of Rome.

King Arthur did them all knightly honour, for he had the bodies embalmed and wrapped in cloth of Sendal and placed in leaden chests with all the shields and arms and banners atop, and he sent them to Rome before his coming. In triumph, at the head of the British army, he entered that ancient city and was crowned Emperor by the Pope himself.

But wonderful as it all was, King Arthur longed for the fair fields of his homeland and so also did his knights.

"We will return again to our castles and our people," he said, and cheer after cheer broke out from the throats of his warriors.

So they all turned their faces again to the land beyond the Channel and set sail once more for home. And thus ended the great campaign which King Arthur undertook against the Emperor Lucius of Rome, which brought to him much honour and glory.

CHAPTER 8

SIR LAUNCELOT

AFTER the great battle, when King Arthur and the Knights of the Round Table were once more back in England, many jousts and tournaments were held. All the knights strove to be the best, and they so improved in arms and honour that they were soon the finest body of men known in any age. But far above them all was Sir Launcelot. Gentle and brave, handsome and chivalrous, he was a pattern of true knighthood, and no one was ever found who could overcome him in combat except by enchantment or deceit. Everyone loved him, and King Arthur and Queen Guinevere held him in great honour. For his Queen's sake he did many knightly deeds of arms. He stayed in Camelot a long while, taking part in the jousts, so that the blazon of his armour came to be well known; it was feared by the craven and the cruel, for Sir Launcelot went about righting wrongs whenever he found them, and with his strength and prowess he was an ill man to deal with. But he grew tired of the court life, his adventurous spirit thirsting after new fields of endeavour.

To one of the other knights, Sir Lionel, he came one hot summer noon when even the court greyhounds lay down panting, too hot to sleep. Bees buzzed and droned in Queen Guinevere's herb-garden.

"Let us away and seek adventure," Sir Launcelot said. "This life is pleasant enough, but I have had enough of idleness. Get you your horse and come with me! We will see what we can find to do."

So, while the other knights either slept or played the lute with the court ladies in the great hall, Sir Launcelot and Sir Lionel donned all their armour and mounted their war horses. Then, with hooves ringing on the drawbridge planks, they left the castle and rode through sleeping Camelot.

"Let us turn into the forest," Sir Launcelot suggested. "Who knows what adventure we may find there!"

But the forest was deserted and when they had ridden through it and come out into the blaze of sunshine again it seemed hotter than ever.

"Not for the past seven years have I known so hot a day nor felt so sleepy," Sir Launcelot said.

"Yes, in such case am I too," Sir Lionel sighed. "See yonder apple-tree. There is thick shade under its branches. Let us lie down there, for we need sleep."

"Well said, brother," agreed Sir Launcelot, and they alighted and led their horses to a pleasant cool spot and tied them to trees, where the flies would not trouble them.

Sir Launcelot took off his helm. With this hard pillow for his head he lay down in the grass and almost at once fell asleep. Sir Lionel followed his example. But something wakened Sir Lionel first and he sat up and looked about. At a distance were three knights, riding furiously as if pursued. And soon after came a single knight in hot chase of them, his harness clashing as he galloped.

"That is a fine figure of a man," Sir Lionel whispered in admiration. "Never saw I a better set-up knight nor one so well armoured at all points. His armour is the finest plate that ever I saw."

He leaned on his elbow and saw the pursuing knight overtake and strike the other three down from their horses, one by one, so that they crashed into the bracken and lay still. With shocked

eyes he watched as the victorious knight alighted, took the bridles
from the three horses, and tied the fallen men up. Then he slung
all three bodies across his own horse.

"This must not be," muttered Sir Lionel, who was passing
brave but very rash in thinking that one so young as himself
could have ado with a knight of such prowess.

He glanced at the quiet, noble face of Sir Launcelot. He
feared he might awake him, so, as softly as he might, he
donned his helm and got upon his horse.

"I will essay this knight by myself," he said, and held his
breath at each creak and clink; but Sir Launcelot slept on.

Sir Lionel moved off as quickly as was possible and his horse's
hooves made only soft sounds among the thick leaves. When
he was far enough off he spurred his mount right smartly and
thundered after his quarry.

"Turn thee, turn and defend thee," Sir Lionel called out.

The other knight spurred his horse round so ably that it turned
and faced him, twisting like an eel. If Sir Lionel's heart quailed
when he saw the full figure before him in its armour strong as
a metal tower, eyes flashing from the visor bars, the bodies on
the horse before him held easily, he did not let that stop him.
As a true knight should, he went straight on despite his mortal
fears.

"Defend thee, knight," he cried again and charged.

Alas for hot-headed youth and inexperience, be it upheld
never so high by courage! The stranger's spear struck Sir
Lionel full in the centre of his shield, and so hard was the blow
that he went over his horse's tail and fell almost senseless to the
ground. Hands fumbled about him, binding him, and he was
flung as the others had been across a horse, his own. And so,
with his four prisoners, the stranger rode away into the gloom
of the deepest part of the forest towards a grim fortalice upon
a crag. With bartisan and buttress and sugar-cone turrets, the
castle looked a place of legend.

Sir Launcelot slept on and knew not what had happened.
Riding by the apple-tree came four queens under a green silk
canopy, which was supported on four spears held by four knights,
so that the hot sun should not trouble them. Sir Launcelot's

horse neighed to their horses, and the queens looked to see who might be there.

"A knight sleeping in his armour," whispered Morgan le Fay to her sister queens. "It is Sir Launcelot! No other man has such a comely look. In truth, he is the flower of knights. Look you, I will put an enchantment upon him so that he shall not wake for six hours. I will take him into my castle, and not being able to escape from us, he must choose one of us to be his love, for fain would we all be loved by so peerless a knight, and that I know well!"

So she did, and still sleeping under her spell Sir Launcelot was lifted and laid upon his shield. Two of the accompanying knights took him between them on horseback, and they all rode away.

When he returned to consciousness, Sir Launcelot stared about him in amazement. He had fallen asleep in the afternoon in the warm shade under the apple-tree, but now all was coldly dark. Straw rustled under him as he moved. Faint starlight came in through the barred window and shone, a pale blue-white radiance, on iron chains and staples on dungeon walls.

There came a clashing of bolts, and the door swung open. A pretty little maiden came in with his supper: a bowl of broth and a manchet of bread.

"What cheer, sir knight?" said she.

"Nay, I can hardly say," said Sir Launcelot, smiling at her. "Some spell must have been put upon me, for I fell asleep under an apple-tree and know not how I came here!"

"Take heart!" The little maiden spoke low. "If you are as great a knight as they say, you will not let this happening disturb you. I will try and tell you more tomorrow, but now I must away in haste lest they become suspicious and I be not able to help you."

"Gramercy, little maiden, and goodnight."

So all that night long Sir Launcelot lay there in the cold. With daylight came the four queens, all wonderfully dressed in their very best stiff brocades with vair or ermine and marvellous jewels. They told him straightly that he was helplessly their prisoner and that if he did not obey them he should die in that prison.

"You shall choose one of us to be your love," they said. "Choose now from us: Morgan le Fay, the Queen of Northgalis, the Queen of Eastland, and the Queen of the Out Isles!"

"This is not an easy problem that you set me to solve," said Sir Launcelot, "to choose between you or else to face death in this your dungeon!" There was that in his eagle glance as he spoke that made them quail and look away. "Rather, far rather, would I die here with honour than love one of you!"

Morgan le Fay was furious at this rebuff. "Then you refuse us," she said, "though you would have freedom and rich comfort and be treated like a king?"

"Freedom of body, perhaps," was the answer, "but hardly freedom of spirit. Yes, I do refuse you!"

They left him at that and the door of his prison clanged to behind their rustling draperies. Sir Launcelot went to the window and stood leaning his elbow on the sill looking out at the fair morning landscape and musing. The wind stirred his dark hair and he sighed to think that perhaps he would never more lay lance in rest at some brave tournament or ride through winter woods seeking worshipful adventure. He wondered what had happened to Sir Lionel and if he had fallen victim too to some great peril and if he himself would ever win a way out and go to help him.

Right so came a timid knock and then the heavy door was unbarred. The little maiden came in with a black pudding for his dinner.

"What cheer?" she asked him.

"Never so ill," he said sorrowfully.

"If you will promise me something," she said, one finger on her lips, "I think that I can help you."

"If I can do it, then will I promise right gladly," Sir Launcelot replied, "for to tell the fair truth these queen sorceresses oppress me, for such as they have destroyed many a good knight."

She nodded wisely. "They are very angry with you because you have humiliated them by refusing to have one of them to be your love. Now then, sir knight, first I will tell you how you can help me as you promised. My father is to be in a tournament

next Tuesday and fight against the King of Northgalis, who has
with him, besides his own knights, three of King Arthur's men.
These are so strong that the last time they rode against my
father he was overthrown and shamed and his party put to rout.
Help him, good Sir Launcelot, and I will help you to escape."

"What is your father's name, my child?"

"Sir, he is King Bagdemagus."

"I know him well for a noble knight and I will help him right
happily. Where shall I meet you so that you may lead me to
him?"

"At the Abbey of White Monks," she told him. "Now eat
your dinner, and before tomorrow's dawn, when all the castle
sleeps, I will help you!"

And sure enough before the stars had paled she came. She
was carrying a heavy bunch of keys.

"Let me carry them," whispered Sir Launcelot. "Are there
then so many locks upon me?"

"Twelve," she answered, giving him the bunch. "But you
must let me tell you which is which as we come to the doors."

"That is sooth," he smiled; "else were I likely to mix them.
Come, then; here is a mighty door!"

"And here is a mighty key," she said gaily.

And so they made their way through dungeon door and
guardroom door and inner bailey door and outer bailey door
and many more to the postern gate. And here in a small room
was his armour, which she helped him don. Then she fetched
his destrier, leading him out gently. Sir Launcelot saddled him,
mounted, and took up his lance. In this wise he won out of the
castle of the four queens. Never had he been in greater peril
than at that time. At the last, just as he was about to ride away,
he looked back. There by the postern gate was the slight figure,
watching him wistfully.

"I shall not fail you, by the grace of God," said Sir Launcelot,
who knew that he had much to do and little time in which to
do it. "For, after helping King Bagdemagus, must I seek for
Sir Lionel and go to his help, for certain I am that he is in trouble
sore and awaits my coming!"

CHAPTER 9

TO THE RESCUE

So AT the time appointed Sir Launcelot made his way to the Abbey and rode beneath its ivied walls. The hooves of his great horse struck sparks from the stones and made such a sound that the daughter of King Bagdemagus, who was waiting for him, heard, and went to the window and looked down.

"It is he, it is the peerless knight!" she said softly and her eyes were shining. Quickly she sent a serving man to take the knight's horse and to unarm him and provide him with a robe. "And I will come as soon as he is comfortable," she promised, and flew to the silver mirror to tidy her curls. Then down the grim stone stairway she crept like a little sunbeam sliding along a churchyard wall. "You are the knight that I can truly welcome more than any in the world," she told him, and put her little hand in his. He had to bend down his proud head to catch her whisper. "I have sent for my father," she went on, "and here he comes!"

Then there was a rattling of hooves on cobbles and there came King Bagdemagus and many good knights with him. As soon as the two men looked in each other's eyes they knew that they could trust each other, for they were as two swords beaten from the same white-hot metal. They embraced, and then Sir Launcelot told King Bagdemagus how his daughter had saved him and how anxious he was to do something in return.

"Now as to this tourney," he went on, "your daughter tells me you are sadly overmatched in numbers."

"That is so," said King Bagdemagus. "The tournament is to be held only three miles from this abbey and already the workmen are building the stands where the people are to sit and watch. They are in a hurry, for Tuesday is nearly upon us."

"Send me three knights of yours whom you can trust utterly," said Sir Launcelot. "Let their shields be plain white with all the blazon painted out, and send one extra such shield for me, and so we will be four knights of mystery who shall come in when no one waits for us and will turn the tide of the combat."

"It shall be done," said King Bagdemagus joyfully. "For certes, as I stand here, I shall be no match against the strength they bring against me unless a good friend such as you help me!"

Tuesday morning dawned passing fair, and from far and near came the horse litters with the queens and ladies, while knights and barons rode with archers and men-at-arms alongside.

Sir Launcelot and the three knights with white shields hid in a little leafy glade hard by. The trumpets rang out their summons enough to stir the heart's blood of even a craven. Then came, prancing and curveting, with beating hooves and flash of inlaid plate, the band of knights of the King of Northgalis, with him at their head. This was the opposing party that should fight with King Bagdemagus, and it was a passing strong party, for there were, all told, one hundred and sixty knights. The three knights of King Arthur who were on the same side as the King of Northgalis rode a little apart, and they were Sir Mador, Sir Mordred and Sir Gahalantine.

King Bagdemagus and his party rode forth, and they were only eighty strong.

They all laid their spears in rest while the horses tramped and jostled and neighed together. Then like two thundering walls of steel the two forces came together and so fought and drew off. Six of the King of Northgalis's party were unhorsed, but so were twelve of King Bagdemagus's.

"It is time for us to ride between them," said Sir Launcelot, and he led out his tiny band and they galloped into the thickest of the fray. And, after his coming, there was no doubt in any man's mind what would happen at the final reckoning, for Sir Launcelot with one lance smote down five knights. He met the King of Northgalis face to face and unhorsed him so that he broke his thigh. The three knights of King Arthur's court marked all this and were dismayed.

"That man is a very hardy fighter," said Sir Mador. "Quickly, let us subdue him, before he swings the fate of the battle against us."

He galloped to Sir Launcelot, his spear steady as a rock, his head and shoulders held low so that the plumes floated out like smoke upon the wind. And Sir Launcelot smiled and met him and overmatched him, for Sir Mador flew out of his saddle as if he were a feather. Then came Sir Mordred, and he, being a better knight, did manage to splinter his lance upon Sir Launcelot's white shield, but he got such a buffet in return that he too fell and his helm was forced into the soft ground by the impact so that it was a wonder his neck did not break. Then Sir Launcelot and Sir Gahalantine broke their spears on each other and took to their swords, but Sir Gahalantine's horse took fright at the fury and dash of the combat and ran away and spilled its master out of his saddle.

Sir Launcelot rode to the barrier for a new spear, and it was such a mighty one that only he could bear it; before it too broke in his hand sixteen knights had gone down before it. Then he took a new spear and unhorsed twelve knights, some of whom limped after that tournament to the end of their days.

At last the knights of the King of Northgalis gave up the fight and would joust no more, so the prize was awarded to King Bagdemagus. He and his daughter thanked Sir Launcelot most joyfully for his help to them and he also thanked her again for his rescue.

"Now must I away to see if I can find where Sir Lionel went," he said, "for it was passing strange that I saw him no more after that we had both fallen asleep under the apple-tree."

Then he told King Bagdemagus's daughter that if ever he might serve her, she having need of a stout arm and ready lance to do some duty for her, she had but to send for him. And so they parted, and he rode his ways from that place straight back to the grim, darkling wood where first he was taken. He talked to any whom he met and found out strange things. Hard by was a tree and on it hung a metal basin and many, many shields belonging to knights who had been overcome by one of the strongest, stoutest knights in all that land; it was he who had carried off Sir Lionel. When any knight beat upon the basin with his spear as a signal, then this knight, whose name was Sir Turquine, came riding down from his castle to have ado with him.

"Alack!" cried Sir Launcelot when he saw the shields hung there, for there were many that he knew, some fresh, some with the blazon weather-dulled as if they had been there many a weary week while their brave owners pined in dungeon darkness. Among the shields was Sir Lionel's.

Then Sir Launcelot went up to the copper basin, and so wrathful was he that he beat upon it till it split and the bottom fell out. He waited long, but no one came. Then he rode up to the castle and up and down before its grim gates for half an hour, watching for some sign of life from turret or wall or bartisan. But all was still. And then at length he saw a knight riding out from the forest, driving another horse before him, and on this second horse lay an armed man, bound.

"It is Sir Gaheris who has been overthrown and captured," Sir Launcelot mused. Aloud he hailed Sir Turquine. "Fair knight, put down that prisoner and let him rest awhile. We two will run a course together and prove our strength, for they tell me that you have done great harm and shame to the Knights of the Round Table!"

"The Table Round!" sneered the other. "I defy you and all your bragging fellowship, for I am a greater knight than any of the four and sixty of your friends who are now in my dungeons. In there they will remain, for I am strong and unless some better man forces me I will not give them up."

"You have said too much already," said Sir Launcelot. "Now will I make you swallow all these boasts!"

He laid his spear in rest and rode against Sir Turquine, but for once he found a man almost as strong as himself, for both their horses were killed with the shock of that meeting and both men were flung from their saddles. But they leaped up again lightly and began to fight with swords. For two hours they fought, round and round, till the grass was trampled and reddened, and so well matched were they that neither could gain advantage. At last they leaned on their swords to rest awhile and they looked upon each other fierce as hawks, their eyes glinting behind their visor bars.

"Tell me," said Sir Turquine, "who you are, for never have I met a man who could withstand me, and much pleasure have you given me in this brave encounter. As long as you are not one man whom I hate above all others, I will, for sheer love of you, set free all the men I hold. And we two will be brothers in arms and do all manner of knightly deeds together and never fail one or the other!"

"Well spoken," said Sir Launcelot. "But first tell me, who is this man whom you hate so grimly, and why?"

"He is called Sir Launcelot and he slew my brother, Sir Carados, at the dolorous tower, and if I meet with him ever he and I shall fight till one of us is finished. And because of him and what he did, I have killed a hundred knights and maimed as many, and many have died in my prisons, nothing availing them!"

"Then defend thyself anew," answered Sir Launcelot lightly, "for that man am I!"

Then they rushed together again and fought and fought through that long summer day until at the last Sir Launcelot slew Sir Turquine and so ended the matter. Then he freed Sir Gaheris.

"Brother, will you lend me your horse so that I may ride on," he asked him, "while you unlock the dungeon doors and let out our fellows of the Round Table and all others who have fallen on evil days because of Sir Turquine?"

"Take my horse? Nay, take all I have," said Sir Gaheris warmly. "You saved me and my horse and so I reckon that all I have is yours, for you are the best knight in all the world, and I say it true. I pray you tell me your name, for I know you not, though always from now on I shall know you, for no man that ever breathed gave such strokes or wielded such a lance."

"I but did my duty, so speak not of it, but hasten to free our fellows," said Sir Launcelot. "Among them is Sir Lionel, for I saw his shield, and also that of Sir Ector de Maris. Greet them all from me and ask these last two to await me at Camelot, where I shall come later. But there are deeds of rescue that I must do, and I have no time to tarry."

Then Sir Launcelot told Sir Gaheris who he was, and after that he rode away. Sir Gaheris went to the porter's lodge at the castle and there he got the keys of the dungeons. Down he strode into damp and rat-haunted cells below ground-level, where daylight slanted seldom in, and there he unlocked door after door and freed the captives until there were none left in durance. And he told them of all the noble deeds of Sir Launcelot and they marvelled extremely.

But Sir Ector de Maris and Sir Lionel would not obey him and hasten to the court.

"What?" they cried. "Shall we let him ride away from us into peril and not seek to help him? We will follow him."

"And I too will come," said Sir Kay; for Sir Gaheris had told them how Sir Launcelot was now riding on new knight-errantry.

All the sixty-four freed knights found each his own horse and his arms and all his gear and they left that grim castle and rode away, free men once more.

CHAPTER 10

BORROWED ARMS

SIR LAUNCELOT did many brave deeds after this, for he freed captive ladies, slew giants, and helped everyone whom he met who was in distress. Sometimes when darkness fell he found lodging in some castle; sometimes he lay out under the stars with his helm for pillow. One day he reached a very wild part of the country, where there were few castles, and seldom could he find shelter or supper for himself and his horse. So he was doubly glad upon coming to a good-sized house where an old dame, taking pity on him, asked him in.

"Take you in? Certes I were a poor thing indeed if I turned away a brave knight," she shrilled. "Take the horse round to the back and tie him up in the shelter. There is corn and water there for him. Then come in and sup with me!"

And she hastened and made right good cheer, and broiled some fowls and broached some wine. They chatted together all the evening, and at last she showed him to a fair room over the entrance gate. There she said goodnight.

Sir Launcelot put his candle down and slowly unarmed himself, for he was passing tired. The bed was much more comfortable than the hard ground on which he had slept so often lately, and he fell sound asleep. He woke to hear a great thunder of knocking upon the gate, so he arose and looked out of the window. Brilliant cold moonlight showed him a man in armour hammering on the oak for admittance, and three knights who were coming upon him fast as if they had been chasing him. All three attacked him at once with their swords and he fought back bravely.

"That is a shame," thought Sir Launcelot. "Three on one! I will see if I may not make it a little more even."

As quickly as he could he armed himself and let himself down out of the window by a sheet.

"Turn from that knight and have ado with me," he called in a great voice as he slid down to them.

They stared in surprise, then left Sir Kay, for it was he, and came rushing to do battle with Sir Launcelot, who was soon fighting strongly with them. Sir Kay put his shield before him and came running to help him, but Sir Launcelot cried out joyously: "Nay, leave them to me, for so I wish it. I do not need your help!"

"Very well," said Sir Kay, and he stood back and watched in admiration the skill of those mighty strokes and the cool confidence of the knight who dealt them.

Sir Launcelot was victorious and forced the three men to the ground by the sheer weight of his onslaught.

"We yield, we yield!" they cried.

"I will not take it," he said. "Yield you to Sir Kay here if you will."

"To Sir Kay? No, never," one cried, "for we were chasing him and would soon have overcome him but for you. The thing is not reasonable."

"You may please yourselves," said Sir Launcelot. "You wish to die, then?"

"No, no! If we can only live on these conditions, then will we yield to Sir Kay," they said.

Sir Launcelot sent them straight off to Camelot to take Sir Kay's greetings to the court.

"And now," he said to his brother knight, "we will go back into shelter again!" He raised his sword and hammered anew at the gate. Presently there was a shuffling within and a trailing wisp of candlelight and the old woman came to unbar the door.

"Mercy on us!" she cried when she saw Sir Launcelot. "I thought you were in bed and asleep!"

"So I was," he smiled, "but I got out of the window to help an old friend of mine."

"Sir Launcelot, it is you!" cried Sir Kay, when the candlelight fell on his deliverer's features. And he thanked him very heartily for all he had done.

The old dame, who liked well having company, was much pleased to have two knights lodging in her house. So she brought cold meat and wine and Sir Kay had his supper and then went aloft to share Sir Launcelot's bed.

Sir Launcelot was awake first the next morning, and as he viewed the sleeping face of Sir Kay his eyes twinkled with fun.

"Ah, Sir Kay," he thought to himself, "hast had a hard time lately, good Sir Kay—first imprisoned by our worthy foe, Sir Turquine, and then set upon by three knights. You shall ride back to Camelot all unharmed and without hindrance!"

So saying, Launcelot carefully picked out Sir Kay's armour and put it on himself. He left his own with its dread and well-known blazoning beside the sleeping knight.

"You canst not ride to Camelot in under-jupon and breeches," he said lightly. "Therefore wear my harness you must!"

So, after thanking his hostess Sir Launcelot rode away, and when Sir Kay woke it happened even as planned.

"But, oh," cried Sir Kay, "many a poor foolish knight will rue this day, for they will think that he is I and will ride against him and there will be many a sore head, I doubt it not."

On his way back to Camelot, Sir Launcelot passed through a thick forest and he saw four knights there and they were of King Arthur's court. They were Sir Ector de Maris, Sir Sagramour, Sir Gawaine and Sir Uwaine. They looked up and saw a knight riding, and of course they imagined it was Sir Kay.

"Now we will prove Sir Kay's might," laughed Sir Sagramour and he snatched up his spear.

Sir Launcelot recognised all of the four and he thought he would surprise them, so he laid his spear in rest and they came together. Down went Sir Sagramour and his horse, and the other three knights opened their eyes.

"That was a shrewd buffet," said Sir Ector de Maris. "That is a much bigger man than Sir Kay ever was. Now you shall watch me and I will essay him. Pass me my spear, I prithee!"

And he galloped down the glade to meet Sir Launcelot. But alas for high hopes! Down went Sir Ector de Maris just as had Sir Sagramour, and Sir Launcelot's spear was still unbroken.

Sir Uwaine looked very serious. "That is a man to be reckoned with," he said. "I know exactly what has happened. He has killed Sir Kay and taken his armour, for well I wot he is not Sir Kay. Now I am going to try myself against him, but I have little hope."

Sir Launcelot swung round to face him as he came. "Ha, Sir Uwaine now," he muttered under his breath. "If I cannot give you a buffet such as shall astonish you I shall be astonished myself."

And it happened just as he had reckoned. Sir Uwaine lay quite a long time in the heather before he could rise; he was so stunned. It was now Sir Gawaine's turn and he did not relish the meeting overmuch, but honour commanded that he should do as the other three had done.

His spear burst into a thousand splinters with the impact and his horse rolled right over him so that he had difficulty in getting free. Like a whirlwind Sir Launcelot passed on.

"God give great joy to the man who made this spear," he said. "I never had a better one and never shall. Well, methinks I will continue on my way, for I do not think these four knights want to see me again!"

So he galloped on up the leafy rides and out of sight. Sir Sagramour, Sir Ector de Maris, Sir Gawaine, and Sir Uwaine comforted each other as best they could and dressed their bruises and saw to their horses. Their heads were still ringing when many hours had gone by.

Two days before the feast of Pentecost, Sir Launcelot got home to Camelot after having many more adventures than can be written down here. King Arthur and Queen Guinevere and all the court were right glad to see him back again. When Sir Sagramour, Sir Ector, Sir Gawaine and Sir Uwaine came riding in and saw him in Sir Kay's armour they knew at once that it had been he who had unhorsed them all with a single spear.

They began to laugh right heartily and Sir Launcelot laughed too and all the court were right merry at the jest. Then came all the knights that had been imprisoned by Sir Turquine and they were loud in their praises of Sir Launcelot and told King Arthur all the tale. Then Sir Kay got up and told them all how he had ridden peacefully home in Sir Launcelot's harness.

"No man would have ado with me!" he said. "One look at this proud shield was enough for them!"

Then came the three knights that had been at the tournament and they told of his prowess. And many others whom Sir Launcelot had vanquished while wearing Sir Kay's armour now came into court and they went straight to Sir Kay to yield them, for he was now in his own harness again. But he shook his head, smiling.

"You never fought with me," he said. "I doubt not that was Sir Launcelot! Yonder he is. Go make your peace with him!"

"Ah, if it was he who overcame us," they said, "we do not mind nor feel so shamed, for who can stand against him?"

So it went abroad through all the land from that day that Sir Launcelot had the greatest name of any knight in all the world and was most honoured of high and low. King Arthur and all his court agreed that it was indeed so.

Sir Launcelot did many other adventures at that time and thought little of them except that they should allow him to be of service to others who were in danger or distress. And if his lance could help them, it was always in readiness, and he feared nothing that ever could come against him.

CHAPTER II

BEAUMAINS RIDES OUT

KING ARTHUR and his court were at the castle of Kynke Kenadonne on the sands near Wales, and there they held the feast of Pentecost one year. Now the King would never sit down to a meal on that day until some unusual happening had taken place.

Sir Gawaine came to him just at midday and told him that he might go to table.

"Three men on horseback and a dwarf are coming across the drawbridge, sire. One of the men is the tallest man with the broadest shoulders that ever I saw. It looks passing strange!"

"Let the food be served," said the King, and he and his knights sat down to meat.

The great doors were flung open and in walked the three men, he of the broad shoulders in the middle.

"The fairest face I have ever seen," said Queen Guinevere. "Why does he lean on those two men with him? They are too richly dressed to be his servants."

"I know not," said King Arthur, with deep interest. "He has the finest hands of any man I know. Methinks he can hold and wield a lance with any here, and yet how white they are! Where is the dwarf?"

"Sire, he is without, holding the horses," said Sir Gawaine.

The good-looking young man came right up to the King's throne and then he straightened up easily enough, for he had no real need to lean on any man. He towered over all present.

"Sire," he said, after he had greeted King Arthur, "I ask three gifts which shall not be more than you can grant, if you so will. The first gift I shall ask for now, and the other two in twelve months' time, at the next feast of Pentecost, wherever you hold it."

King Arthur loved adventure and this promised to be a most interesting happening. "Ask your boon," he said eagerly.

"It is simply this," explained the young man. "Provide me

with food and drink for this coming year and then I will ask my other two gifts!"

The King's face fell, for here was no worshipful mystery, only a commonplace request for food and lodging.

"Son," he said in disappointed tones, "think again, and ask better. I have taken a liking to you and I feel that you will someday be a man with whom all must reckon, so I am prepared to grant much bigger gifts than you ask."

"I have no more to say," said the youth.

"Well, of course I will give you food and drink—I never denied that to anyone, even my foes. But tell me your name, son."

"That I cannot do," was the answer, at which King Arthur and his knights marvelled anew.

"I will speak to my seneschal touching your request," said King Arthur, and he sought out Sir Kay. "Lodge him as a lord's son," he said. "See that he has everything of the richest and best!"

"There is no need to waste your kindness on him," growled Sir Kay. "A crow flies where there is carrion. If he had been of metal true he would have asked horse and arms for to get out and gain worship. He is of common clay, sire, seeking only to stuff himself with pasties and drink your wine!" Sir Kay went on maliciously: "I will put him in the kitchen to live among the cooking and the grease. I'll wager he'll be so fat come next Pentecost he'll not be able to get on a horse, let alone ask for one. No name, has he? Ha! I will call him Beaumains—Fair-hands—and he won't keep them long in the kitchen!"

"I think you are making a mistake," King Arthur said, but he left the matter to Sir Kay.

Sir Gawaine was very angry when he heard, and so was Sir Launcelot.

"I advise you to leave this mockery alone," Sir Launcelot cried when he met Sir Kay in the great hall. "The lad will turn out to be a man of great honour, and then it will be you who will look foolish!"

Sir Kay shook his head. "He was probably brought up in some abbey where the trencher and tankard were oftener empty than full. He yearns for fat meat; fat meat he shall have!"

And Sir Kay put Beaumains among the kitchen lads to eat his supper, and he sat there looking rather sad.

"Come to my chamber," said Sir Launcelot, looking very kindly on the young man. "Come and eat with me and bear me company."

Beaumains shook his head. "I thank you, fair lord, but it is all part of this adventure," he said, "that I should do as Sir Kay bids me."

And so also he answered Sir Gawaine when he tried to make up to him for his harsh treatment. Sir Gawaine was drawn to him, but he knew not that the reason was that it was his own brother grown to man's estate since he himself left his home to go out into the world. But Sir Launcelot had no such unconscious reason; what he did was from his natural chivalry and honour.

Day after day, through the hot summer and chilling autumn and bleak winter, Beaumains lived in the kitchen by day, and at night he lay down to sleep upon the warm hearth among the ashes, as did the common boys. And they all loved him, for no matter how trying anyone was, his high courage and noble disposition carried him through all storms and troubles.

When the knights jousted, Beaumains went to watch. His flushed cheeks and kindling eyes suggested that such things were more truly part of him than broth-kettles and roasting-spits. Sir Launcelot gave him gold to spend and rich clothes to wear and so did his brother, but Sir Kay changed not. When there was a trial of strength among the young squires, shooting or throwing stones, Beaumains would outdo them all.

Launcelot, watching with secret pleasure as the young man succeeded in outdoing all the others, glanced across at Sir Kay, and there was condemnation in his look.

Sir Kay merely shrugged. "So you like my kitchen-boy, do you?" he laughed.

The court moved to Carlion for the feast of Pentecost that year and, as usual, King Arthur put off eating anything on that day until some strange adventure happened. They soon told him, however, that he could sit down at table, for a most beautiful damosel was riding up the winding valley road to the castle.

c

This lovely lady came into the hall, and very fair she was. She was dressed in sea-green silk, and her corn-coloured plaits of hair reached to her knees.

"King Arthur," she cried, "I ask your help."

"For whom?" asked the King.

"Oh, sire, there is a lovely lady besieged in her own fortalice so that she cannot ride forth to hawk or hunt or see her friends, for a wicked tyrant has pitched his camp below her walls. I have ever heard that your knights are the noblest in the world, so hither I am come to ask for a brave and doughty hero who will ride against this tyrant and free my lady."

"What is her name, fair damosel?" King Arthur asked.

"I cannot tell you that just now," she replied, "but she is of high worship and renown, but the name of the tyrant is the Red Knight of the Red Lawns."

"I do not know that name," mused the King.

Sir Gawaine spoke up. "I know him well! I have cause to remember him, for from him I escaped only just with my life. He is one of the most dangerous men who ever couched lance or rode to joust."

"It is not enough," said the King justly. "As you will not be open with me and tell me your lady's name I cannot send any of my knights to help you!"

There was a stir by the door from the great stone kitchens and Beaumains strode into the hall. The young man was not a pound fatter than a year ago, but he looked tougher and stronger than ever, with muscles of steel. He had the face of a Greek god, and a proud and knightly bearing.

"Noble King," said Beaumains, "I must now thank you for taking me in and housing and feeding me these twelve months long. Now do I ask once again for boons—the remaining two."

"Ask," said King Arthur, and all the knights looked at one another, for they began to see where this thing was heading.

"Give me this adventure," Beaumains said simply. "It belongs to me."

King Arthur looked at the goodly young man and nodded. "I grant it! What of your other boon?"

"I would be made knight of Sir Launcelot and no one else, and I ask you to bid him ride after me and give me the great order of knighthood when I shall ask it."

"It shall be so," said the King.

But now the lady broke in. She was pale with fury and her eyes flashed like stars. "Shame, shame on you, noble King. I ask for a knight to succour my lady and you send a kitchen-boy with his hands still slimy with grease from the cooking-pots. Varlets, bring me my horse again. The sooner I leave this place the better, or I may say something in my anger that ill beseems me!"

So the damosel mounted and galloped away. But even as she went, a squire came hurrying to exclaim breathlessly to Beaumains that the dwarf was at the postern gate with his gear, harness and horse and all that he needed.

"And of the richest material that ever you saw," gasped the squire. "There are jewels in the hilt of the sword and gold thread in the saddle cloth and carved gold upon the chamfrain."

"From whence came all that gear?" the knights inquired.

When Beaumains had donned the rich inlaid armour, he clanked into the hall and took leave of King Arthur, kneeling bareheaded before him, and he looked one of the finest knights that ever had placed his hands in fealty between those of his overlord. Then he mounted and rode after the damosel. King Arthur and his knights stood below the portcullis and watched him depart.

"It worries me much," said the King, "that with all that goodly harness he has neither shield nor spear!"

Sir Kay smiled sourly. "Bring me my horse," he commanded a squire. "I will ride after my kitchen-boy to taunt him!"

Sir Launcelot, who was preparing to follow at a distance as he had promised, whirled fiercely on Sir Kay. "Stay you at home and do no more damage," he told him sternly.

But Sir Kay would not listen, and he galloped after Beaumains and overtook him just as he overtook the damosel.

"Beaumains, do you not know me?" jeered Sir Kay, and the other man turned his horse.

"Yes, Sir Kay," he answered calmly. "I know you for a most ungentle knight!"

At that, Sir Kay laid his spear in rest and charged down upon Beaumains, forgetting in his petty anger the knightly laws of fair play, for Beaumains sat his horse defenceless, having no shield or spear. But he was daring and bold, and so he drew his sword and charged at Sir Kay, whirling the steel about his head. With one mighty stroke he dashed aside Sir Kay's spear and wounded him so that he fell off his horse in a faint. Beaumains then dismounted and took Sir Kay's shield and spear. Bidding his dwarf mount Sir Kay's horse, he rode on after the lady.

Sir Launcelot sat his horse and watched it all and a grim little smile twisted his lips. The lady had seen it all too, but her nose was turned up in disdain. She turned her horse and rode on. Sir Launcelot overtook Beaumains.

"Will you joust with me?" Beaumains asked hopefully and Sir Launcelot agreed.

They charged upon each other so fiercely that both were thrown from their horses. Sir Launcelot was up first and helped Beaumains away from his kicking mount. Then they continued the fight on foot. So well and so fiercely did Beaumains fight, strong as a boar and quick as a levin flash, that Sir Launcelot began to wonder ruefully if he was going to be beaten to his knees for the first time in his life.

"Beaumains," he begged, "fight not so sore! There is no quarrel between us; we do but try our mettle.. Think you we might leave off now?"

"That is truth," Beaumains answered. "But that bout has done me good. It is wonderful to feel your mighty strength, Sir Launcelot, and yet—I must say—I had not called on all my reserve!"

"Well, I had all I could do not to be shamed, so I cannot see that you need fear to fight with any man!"

"Then do you think that I could prove a goodly knight?" Beaumains asked wistfully.

"Yes, if you fight as you did just now," he was answered.

A light spread over Beaumains's young face. "Then make me a knight," he asked humbly.

Sir Launcelot looked on him kindly. "Then must you tell me your name and of what kin you are born."

"You will not tell anyone?" Beaumains asked.

"Not till you wish it."

So then Beaumains said that he was of royal blood, and his name was Gareth, son of King Lot of Orkney and brother to Sir Gawaine. Sir Launcelot was overjoyed, for he knew that he had been right all along in thinking that the man before him would prove himself, and rise to greatness and worship.

"Kneel!" he commanded, and he touched him with his sword and made him knight. Then they went each his own way and Sir Launcelot took up Sir Kay's senseless body and brought him back to Carlion, where he lay a long time getting better and perhaps regretting that he had not been more courteous and gentle.

Beaumains spurred his horse and rode after the damosel, but he was received with contempt.

"Keep away from me," she told him scornfully. "You smell of the kitchen. And think not that I am going to praise you for overcoming that knight, Sir Kay, for you gave him a coward's blow! What are you but a turner of roasting-spits and a dish-washer? How should you know any better what becomes a gentle knight? Do not follow me any farther, for I will not have your service!"

Beaumains shook his head. "Nay," he said; "I shall ride with you even as I said for to succour your lady. I will finish this adventure or die doing my duty!"

"Fie!" sneered the damosel. "You will soon meet knights who will make your boasts as useless as they are empty."

"Still shall I go on," said Beaumains simply.

CHAPTER 12

THE DEEDS OF SIR BEAUMAINS

THEY rode on in silence for a while, the dwarf bringing up the rear on Sir Kay's horse. Then they saw a man running towards them as fast as he could.

"Oh, gentle sir, help me," the man begged. "Six wicked thieves have set upon my master and bound him to kill him. This way, pray—hasten!"

Sir Beaumains spurred his horse and there in a clearing was the knight bound and helpless and the six men just going to hew off his head. Sir Beaumains charged upon them, shouting to them to desist. With three strokes he killed three of the men and, seeing this, the other three fled screaming. But he galloped after them and killed them too. Then he returned and set the knight free.

"Thanks, gracious sir," said the knight. "Ride with me to my castle and pass the night," he then urged, but Sir Beaumains shook his head.

"I must ride with this damosel," he said.

So the knight rode to the lady, who sat scornfully upon her horse and cried to Sir Beaumains not to come near, for he smelt of grease.

"Ride to my castle with me and I will make you right good cheer," the knight said.

It was darkening for night and blowing up cold, and the forest looked lonesome, so the lady said she would. But when they were sitting down to meat she saw that the knight had placed Sir Beaumains before her and she was extremely cross.

"That wretch is fit only for pig-killing in the castle yard," she scolded. "And you have set him above a lady of noble peerage!"

"Sit at the side table," the knight whispered to Sir Beaumains. "It will make less trouble!" But he was amazed at her treatment of so good a knight.

Next morning early Sir Beaumains and the damosel thanked their host and rode out again and came to a wide river with but one ford across it. Sitting on their horses like grim sentinels on the far bank were two armed men. It was evident that they meant to try and stop anyone from getting across.

"Now," said the damosel with a malicious smile, "you had better turn back and not try to match these knights!"

"I should not turn away if there were six of them," Sir Beaumains answered calmly. He spurred his noble horse down into the river and so began riding across, the water splashing up like great fans on each side of him and sparkling in the sun.

One of the knights at once did the same. They met in midstream and each broke his spear into splinters. Out came swords, and a terrific combat began for the right of way over the river, but Sir Beaumains was a better fighter and he cleared the way of both men. Then he returned to the lady and told her it was clear for her to ride on.

"It makes me angry," she stormed, "that a mere kitchen-boy should have slain two noble knights. Yet it was merest chance. The first man's horse stumbled and so he fell and was drowned, and the other was struck a lucky blow."

Sir Beaumains looked on her quietly. "Say what you will," he replied. "I do not care so long as I can win through to save your lady!"

So all that day they rode and all the time the lady mocked and spoke meanly to Sir Beaumains, but he suffered it and would not leave her. As the sun was slanting to the west they came to a black-burned heath where grew a spectral-looking blackthorn on which hung a black shield, and there was a black knight in black harness beside it.

"Now fly, Beaumains," advised the lady. "Quickly, before he sees you to come at you!"

"Thank you," was the cool answer. "You ever seem to want me to play a coward part."

"It is too late," she said sullenly; "he rides to meet us."

"Damosel," cried the black knight, "is this the knight from King Arthur's court you sought as champion?" For, to speak sooth, Sir Beaumains was a seemly-looking knight, well armed and in rich harness.

"*This?*" she replied cuttingly. "This is a kitchen-boy!"

"And he is dressed like that? It shames you that he bears you company!"

"I cannot be rid of him," she said coldly. "He has killed two knights today, but 'twas by merest chance."

"I am surprised that any honourable man would have ado with a kitchen-boy," sneered the black knight. "Still, he looks a strong enough fellow. I will put him off his horse and take his harness. More than that I cannot do with honour against a menial!"

"Sir knight," said Beaumains gently, "you are very quick in deciding what you will do with my harness. I intend to go on this road over the heath, so you had better clear out of my way."

At that the black knight spurred down upon him and they fought right fiercely, but again Beaumains was the better man and he slew the black knight. He took his armour and donned it, leaving his own, and rode after the damosel.

"Keep away, kitchen-boy," she warned him. "You may have killed that good and gallant knight, but still you are only a spit-turner and you smell of the baking-oven."

He said nothing, but rode on beside her on his errand. Soon they came to a green knight, he in green harness and his horse in green trappings, very wondrous to see. The green knight hailed the lady.

"Is that my brother, the black knight, who rides with you?"

"No," she replied; "this kitchen-knave slew him unfairly."

"Traitor, you shall die for my brother!" said the green knight.

Sir Beaumains shrugged. "I defy you," he said, "and understand that I killed your brother fairly and with no unknightly blow!"

"Defend thee," cried the green knight, and charged.

They broke their spears, but both remained in the saddle; so they fell to fighting with swords. Sir Beaumains's horse sidled up against the green knight's mount and overthrew it, so he went tumbling off. But he sprang to his feet and rushed upon Sir Beaumains again on foot. Seeing this, Sir Beaumains also alighted and they went on fighting fiercely.

Then the lady drew near and taunted the green knight: "It is shame to you, sir knight, that you cannot overcome him."

At this, the green knight heaved up his sword and split Sir Beaumains's shield in two, but Sir Beaumains dealt him such a buffet in return that he went down with a crash.

"Mercy!" begged he. "I yield myself. Slay me not."

"You shall live if this lady pleads for you," said Sir Beaumains between his teeth.

"Fie, false kitchen-boy," she cried. "I shall never plead with you for anything."

"Then he dies!" said Sir Beaumains.

"Fair lady, suffer me to live. A word from you will save me," begged the green knight.

Beaumains made as if to cut off his head, at which the lady could bear no more.

"Let be with your killing," she commanded.

"Your wish is my pleasure," said her knight-errant. "Knight of the green harness, you are free from me!"

Then did the green knight kneel and do homage with his sword, and he promised that he himself and thirty knights of his would be at Sir Beaumains's call whenever it should please him, and he was thanked and told that he should be summoned to King Arthur's court.

"It is a scandal," sneered the lady, "that brave men should obey a greasy lout!"

Then the green knight took them to his manor and made them good cheer, but still the lady spoke meanly to her champion.

"Why do you talk to him so?" asked the green knight. "He is a noble man and I know of none who can match him. It will be proved, mark my words, that he comes of king's blood."

When they were all retired for the night, the green knight crept out and set his thirty men to guard Sir Beaumains lest evil should come to him. And in the morning they all breakfasted and rode on their ways, and the green knight conducted them through a perilous forest and set them on the right road.

Then, in like manner that day, they met with a red knight, and as it fell out before, so it fell out again. Sir Beaumains was the victor and he made the damosel plead for the red knight's life, which she did with an ill grace. But the red knight was an honourable man, and, as he had yielded to Sir Beaumains, he promised that he and sixty of his knights should wait upon King Arthur to do him homage, as he was bidden.

So, after accepting the red knight's hospitality for the night, Sir Beaumains and the lady and the dwarf rode on again; but still she chided him in the cruellest way.

Approaching a great city, the lady began as usual to sneer.

"Fly now while you have time," she advised. "The knight that jousts in the meadow before this city is called Sir Persant of Inde and such a man as he is ye have not yet met. He and his five hundred knights are invincible!"

"This brave knight I should like to meet," said Sir Beaumains, unabashed. "If he is as noble as you say he will not set on me with all five hundred knights at once, and if they come one at a time I can manage!"

Then at last the lady blushed and hid her face for shame, and was sorry.

"You must be of high renown and great honour," she said humbly. "No kitchen-knave could talk as you do or bear with me as knightly as you have done. Pray forgive me!"

"I do right heartily," said Sir Beaumains, his face bright with pleasure that he had overcome her malice. "And, indeed, lady, you did me service, for each time you spoke me ill you made me angry and I felt that I could fight anything; so did I vent my wrath on the knights we met. Let us forward and meet this Sir Persant, for I suppose I shall be able to overcome him!"

And so he did, and this time the lady pleaded for Sir Persant's life without being asked. Afterwards they all repaired to his pavilion, and there they were rested and feasted nobly, and Sir Persant, the blue knight, promised fealty to King Arthur with a hundred of his men. While they sat at meat, he asked the damosel where she and her knight-errant were riding, and she told him, to save her sister, the Lady Liones, who was besieged by the Red Knight of the Red Lawns, which was the most perilous knight in all those parts.

So Sir Beaumains learned that his lady's name was Linet. Then did he tell them that he was the son of the King of Orkney, that Sir Gawaine was his brother, that his real name was Sir Gareth, and that Sir Launcelot had made him knight. She was passing glad to hear all this.

At last they came to a fair castle on a plain, and it was so beautiful that it was as an ivory toy set upon green velvet, for its walls were of white stone and its towers and turrets tiled with copper. A lonesome sea washed the walls of the castle upon the one side, and all manner of strange ships plied to and fro. But the mariners cried out at the ropes and it was as if they sang dolorously. On all the green trees on the green velvet plain swung the bodies of brave knights dead, all slain by the Red Knight of the Red Lawns when they tried to succour the Lady Liones. This knight was a very strong and brave man, but a ruthless one, and he used such shameful customs that he was feared far and near. Famous blazons on famous shields were there, and the spurs on the dead men's heels were all of gold and all the arms were very rich.

For the first time on this adventure, Sir Beaumains's face fell and he looked shocked to see such ruthless butchery, but Lady Linet strove to cheer him.

"Take heart, good knight," she said, "else are we all lost, for all our hope is now in you, and doubt not my sister has word we are coming to her rescue and watches us even now from her window. Take heart, Sir Gareth!"

So Sir Gareth squared his shoulders. "I will win honour this day," he promised her, "or die like a true knight on the field of battle."

CHAPTER 13

SIR BEAUMAINS RETURNS

THEN did the damosel Linet point out to Sir Gareth a horn made from an elephant's tusk, which hung in a sycamore tree.

"That is to summon the Knight of the Red Lawns. He will come and fight whoso shall blow it. But do not touch it till high noon, for men say his strength wanes then, but in the morning, as it is now, it waxes!"

"For shame," he reproached her. "Shall I then seek the easy path?" And he spurred up to the tree and blew the horn mightily.

From all the tents and pavilions men came rushing to stand and watch, and the castle ramparts were black with the people leaning over the walls to see what great deeds might be at hand.

"Ah, look, there he comes," said Linet, as a horseman galloped out from the castle yard. "But look also, good Sir Gareth, there at an upper turret window is my sister for whom you fight!"

He looked, and there he beheld the loveliest lady he had ever seen. Her hair was as the gold of sunrise and her eyes were the blue of the wild iris, and she was clad in cloth of silver. And, looking at her, he fell deeply in love with her.

"You stare at the window," shouted the Knight of the Red Lawns; "now look at me! 'Twill serve you better. The lady is mine and not for you."

"I love her," said Sir Gareth, "and I will rescue her or die here under her walls."

"Then will you die!" said the Red Knight. "Make you ready and defend yourself."

Both men laid their spears in rest and spurred their gallant steeds. They met at a furious pace, and each struck his opponent exactly in the middle of his shield, so that the harness burst and the saddles slipped and both were hurled to the ground, bridles still entangled in their mailed gloves. So terrible was the fall that both were stunned, and all the onlookers feared they had broken their necks. But they rose at last and put their shields before them and rushed together to strike and hack and hew so that their armour cracked and fell, piece by piece, upon the grass. They fought until they could not take another step for lack of breath, but stood, panting and bleeding, till many who saw them shuddered for pity of them, and the Lady Linet crouched terrified on the grass. The Lady Liones wept sore at the hurts of her champion.

When the two were rested they came together again. Sometimes they ran at one another like two rams charging. From prime till evensong they fought, and men still sing the story of that mighty combat. No one could say which knight would win.

The Red Knight was the cleverest fighter that Sir Gareth had ever met, and many a trick he picked up from him that day, but he bought his knowledge dearly. By mutual consent, when it began to be dusk, they took a rest and set them down upon hillocks. They unlaced their helms so that the evening wind could freshen them with its cold breath. The Red Knight had his page to help him and Sir Gareth had his dwarf.

When his helm was off, Gareth looked up to the turret-window and saw the fair face of his lady, and she smiled at him so gloriously that his heart, which was passing heavy with pain and weariness, became light and joyous.

"Defend you again, sir knight," he cried, "and we will to battle anew!"

Then they laced up their helms and fought again, and first Sir Gareth was down and like to lose, and then the Red Knight. Sir Gareth was about to slay him when he yielded and asked for mercy, and all his people came running and begged Sir Gareth to spare him.

"I cannot do it," said Gareth. "For the shameful deaths you have caused all those noble knights to die you ought yourself to be slain!"

But the Red Knight told him he had done it in revenge for a wronged lady whose brother had been killed by an unknown knight, and he begged so pitifully for mercy that Sir Gareth could not slay him.

"Yield you to the Lady Liones, whom you have besieged for all these weary months, and if she forgives you then will I also," he said.

And so it was, and the Red Knight of the Red Lawns was bound in honour to go to King Arthur's court and give his service.

Then Sir Gareth rode proudly up to the castle gate to do homage to the lady for whom he had taken on this deed of knight-errantry. Across the drawbridge his great destrier stamped, and so, with clanking harness and waving plume, he rode into the castle yard. But the big inner door was shut and bolted against him.

The Lady Liones came to a gallery window and looked down. "Go thy way and ride from this castle," she said, and her voice was sweet and musical. "Go and win more honour, and return here this day twelve-month and then I will answer you differently! But now I shall not give you all my love."

"I have not deserved this hardness," Sir Gareth reproached her. "Have I not won the right to woo you, for I have spilled some of the best blood in my body in your service?"

"Fair knight," sighed the Lady Liones, "be not displeased with me. Twelve months flies soon, so very soon!" And she turned away and would speak no more. In sooth, she wished to make sure first of what blood and kin was this her champion, so for this reason was she so hard.

Gareth's heart was nigh to breaking and he rode away, his faithful dwarf following as always. He rode through briar and brake and wild-rose tangle and marsh and stony vale, and all was the same to him, for he wit not where he went nor how. He slept where he could, but he rested ill, for the vision of the Lady Liones, who was, he believed, lost to him, came before him to torture him.

But in the meantime she sent and stole away his dwarf, for she said: "He will know who his master is!"

Her brother, Sir Gringamore, did the deed and bore the dwarf away when Sir Gareth slept, but he lamented so loudly and screamed so long for help that his master awoke and set out in pursuit.

Sir Gringamore got back to his own castle, where the Lady Linet and the Lady Liones were lodging, and all was gay and merry when they found from the dwarf that Gareth was indeed a king's son and a worthy knight. Then up to the walls stormily rode Sir Gareth, his sword drawn and his countenance dark with anger.

"Traitor knight," he shouted, "give me back my dwarf, or by all I owe to the order of knighthood I will not rest till I have destroyed you!"

Sir Gringamore looked out of a window. "Sir Gareth of Orkney," he cried, "you shall not have your dwarf!"

"Yes, he shall," said the Lady Liones. "The dwarf has told me all that I wanted to know, and my sister says it is indeed so. I will not keep him from his good master."

Sir Gringamore shrugged in disdain at the changing minds of women and right ruefully he went down and himself unbolted the great door.

"I ask your pardon for what I said just now," he cried. "I answered you right shortly, Sir Gareth. Alight and enter and we will make you such cheer as we can!"

"Where is my dwarf?" Sir Gareth demanded.

"He awaits you at this moment," Sir Gringamore said hastily.

So his visitor dismounted and went in, and lo, coming to meet him was his own fair lady of the iris eyes and the silver dress. And they two plighted their troth and kissed one another and their hearts were happy.

Then in came the Lady Linet, who had ridden with Sir Gareth so many perilous miles, and they greeted each other. So all was merry that day in Sir Gringamore's castle on the marches. After a long while Sir Gareth took his leave and prepared to ride back to King Arthur's court, and Sir Gringamore promised to follow and escort the two ladies with him.

Pentecost was drawing near again and King Arthur was getting all in readiness for it, for there would be a great assembly at the court. To him a squire came running, breathless with excitement.

"There is a green knight coming, riding in thunder and dust across the plain to your gates!" he cried. "And with him are thirty bold knights with pennants flying so that it is as if all the ribbons in my lady's basket were spread abroad!"

Into the court they rode and dismounted and came into the King's presence with bare heads, and they knelt and did homage, a wondrous fair sight to see. Right so came another squire, hurrying.

"Sire, sire," he panted, "there is a red knight galloping up to the gate and with him are sixty of the best men who ever donned embroidered coat."

"Let them in," cried King Arthur joyously, and hardly had this company crowded into the hall when a trumpet call without the gates announced another arrival, and, lo, there was the blue knight with one hundred men to yield himself to the King.

Then the three brothers told the King how they had been overcome by a peerless knight called Sir Beaumains, who had given them this command that they should yield to King Arthur.

"I marvel greatly at him," said King Arthur, shaking his head. "Of kings indeed must he be born. He was here for a twelve-month and poorly and shamefully was he treated. It was Sir Kay who dubbed him Beaumains!"

The oak door swung open and there stood Sir Launcelot, proud and noble, as always. "Sire," he said, and his eyes were laughing, "there is a goodly knight at your outer gates and he brings six hundred knights in his train, so that it is a wonder to behold, for so thick do they crowd that you can no longer see the meadow grass beyond the moat."

Then did the King go out to meet this knight and bid him enter into Carlion. He found it was Sir Ironside, the Red Knight of the Red Lawns. And so at last, after years of warring together, all these knights were friends with King Arthur and his men, and all men praised Sir Beaumains for bringing it to pass.

"Where is he now?" the King asked, but Sir Ironside did not know.

Then more trumpets blew, and into the castle yard rode the Queen of Orkney, who had not seen her sons for many years and was come to visit them. They came: Sir Gawaine, Sir Agravaine and Sir Gaheris, and they kneeled before their mother and she blessed them, but ever her bright eyes were roaming about the hall seeking something.

"What have you done with my youngest son Gareth, O my brother?" she said lightly to King Arthur. "He came here, and I heard it said you made a kitchen-boy of him!"

"What?" cried Sir Gawaine, aghast. "Was Beaumains my brother Gareth, whom I last saw climbing about the rocks at Orkney? Alas, alas, and I knew him not!"

"And I knew him not, either, that was my own nephew," said the King. "Woe is me, for Sir Kay treated him shamefully, and now he is gone; but we will amend it. He shall be found again."

So it befell that King Arthur by devious means sought out Sir Gareth and after many days brought him home. Sir Gringamore was true to his promise and rode to court with the two ladies, Liones and Linet, and they were received with great joy.

At Michaelmas of that year was such a wedding at the court that history has never since matched it, for all the kings and queens then living in those parts, and all the great knights and

barons, princes and earls, were there, so that for colour and
pageantry it was never again equalled.

And King Arthur made the red knight, the green knight and the
blue knight knights of the Round Table, and also Sir Ironside, to
be in the fellowship to their lives end. Sir Gareth wedded the Lady
Liones, Sir Gaheris wedded the Lady Linet, and Sir Agravaine
wedded the Lady Laurel; and the Archbishop of Canterbury
solemnised the weddings.

There were great jousts and merry cheer for forty days,
but the newly married knights were not allowed to joust lest
some mishap overtook them and brought sorrow to their lovely
ladies.

So ends the story of Sir Gareth of Orkney, who was a noble
knight and in all he did honourable, gentle of speech, and brave
of heart.

CHAPTER 14

THE STORY OF SIR TRISTRAM

THIS is the story of a great knight who met with many sorrows,
but who, despite them all, lived to be one of the most famous
of his time. His mother died in giving him birth and so he was
called Tristram, which means "born in sorrow".

King Meliodas, his father, married again and Tristram found
his stepmother hard and cruel, for she hated him, wanting her
own children to inherit the country of Liones.

"If I poison young Tristram," the Queen thought, "then my
own son shall be king in time!" This was when the boy Tristram
was about ten years old. "Brew me poison," she whispered to
her secret helper. "Brew it in a drink of wine so that he may
never know that a snake hides within the silver cup!"

So it was done, and the Queen hid the wine in the chamber
where the children played. But young Tristram went out to see
some spearthrowing and it was the Queen's own son who saw the
silver cup.

"I thirst," he said, "and there is a fair wine in this cup." And he drank it.

It was a very potent poison, and at once he sank helpless to the floor.

They took up the poor limp body, and the Queen was beside herself with rage and grief. So overwrought was she that she ordered more poison at once, for now she could not bear to think of Tristram reigning instead of her own dead child.

King Meliodas came in hot from hunting and he strode into the children's room to see if haply young Tristram were there for he loved him dearly. But Tristram was at the tournament ground watching the riding, and the King turned away disappointed. Right so he saw the silver cup and took it up to drain it.

There was a swish of silken draperies, and the Queen rushed in. "No—ah, no—not you too!" she cried, and dashed the cup out of his hand.

The poison spilled upon the marble tiles and bit deeply into them, and it scorched the King's furred mantle so that holes appeared. King Meliodas was quick-witted and he saw it all. He caught her by the hand and looked long and fiercely into her eyes.

"You shall die for this," he exclaimed.

The Queen was tried by the great barons and sentenced to be burnt to death at the stake. The King was sorrowful, but justice must be done to all, to queens as well as commoners. But even more upset was Tristram, who now saw clearer than any why his stepmother had been so cruel to him. And because of his nobility, his heart grieved sore for her. So he went and kneeled before the King and asked a boon. When this was granted, he asked his father that he might go and save the Queen.

King Meliodas, having promised, would not break his word, so Tristram ran down to the great square where the Queen was to die. Her lovely face was streaked with unhappy tears, and she was bound to a stake of green wood. Men were just coming with torches to start the blaze when the boy flung himself between.

"Hold—hold in the King's name! Free the Queen! The King so commands it through me. Let her be loosed!"

So they untied her and she swooned in Tristram's arms; and from that day on she loved him dearly and would have given her life for him. But King Meliodas was determined to get his son away from court influence, and so he sent him to France with his man, Gouvernail, to learn the language and to practise deeds-of-arms.

Tristram was very happy in that fair land for more than seven years. He learned to play the harp so beautifully that even the birds stilled to hear him. In all kinds of outdoor skill, in hunting and hawking and archery, was he peerless, and some of the terms he gave to the sports are yet used. When he returned to Liones in Cornwall he became much loved by all.

Now, in those times, for many long winters past, King Mark of Cornwall had paid tribute to King Anguish of Ireland. King Mark was a cowardly, shiftless, mean knight, and he had fallen behind with his payments for seven years.

"I have not paid all that time," said he, "so why should I take up the matter again? Send a messenger and tell King Anguish so; but—stay—I see a way out of the difficulty. If the King insists on his tribute, tell him to pick a champion and I will send one against him and each shall fight for the rights of his own country!"

King Anguish was wroth when he got the message. He called to him Sir Marhaus, a famous knight of the Round Table, and his own brother-in-law.

"Will you take this thing on yourself?" he asked. "We trust you, brother, as ourself. Whatever expense you are put to shall be more than met."

"I will do it with a right good will," promised Sir Marhaus.

A ship was made ready for him in all haste and laden with all things he should need, and with a fair wind he left Ireland and landed on the coasts of Cornwall hard by the castle of Tintagel.

"Who has come to the challenge?" King Mark asked eagerly, but when he heard his craven heart misgave him. "We have no man who can have ado with *him*," he said.

Sir Marhaus waited in his great ship in the bay and each day he sent to King Mark demanding either the payment of the tribute or else a champion to fight. The people of Cornwall sent about in their towns and castles for a knight to meet Sir Marhaus

and save the payment of the tribute. Great rewards were offered
to the hero when he should appear.

"Send to King Arthur and ask him to lend us Sir Launcelot,"
cried some of the Cornish barons, but some said no, for Sir
Marhaus was himself a knight of the Table Round and they would
be loth to have ado with one another.

Young Tristram of Liones heard how Sir Marhaus stood his
ship defying the whole Cornish realm, and he was ashamed for
his country that no one could be found to meet the knight.

He himself was nineteen at this time, strong and true, the steel
of swords in his level glance. To King Meliodas therefore he went.

"It is a shame to us all!" he said. "If Sir Marhaus sails without
our finding a champion to fight him we shall never have pride
again in our fair land."

King Meliodas nodded mournfully. "True, son Tristram, but
I know no man who could match him. Sir Marhaus is famed
far and near!"

"Woe is me that I am not a knight," said Tristram. "If I
were, I would meet him. Give me leave to ride to King Mark and
offer myself."

"Do as your courage bids you," answered King Meliodas, and
his eyes were proud as he gazed on his fair son.

So to King Mark's rode young Tristram. "Make me knight and
I will meet Sir Marhaus," he said, his head held high.

The King surveyed him gloomily. "Who are you?" he asked
shortly.

"The son of King Meliodas, who married your sister!"

"I will make you a knight," said King Mark hastily, as if
afraid that this golden chance might slip away if he did not
hurry.

"I came for that one reason," Tristram answered calmly.

So King Mark made him a knight and then sent off in haste a
letter to Sir Marhaus to say he had found a champion.

"That is well," Sir Marhaus said, "but I will not fight *anybody*
whom he picks up. He must be of royal blood."

He was assured that it was even so, for the new champion was
the Prince of Liones, King Mark's nephew. The Cornish King
found Sir Tristram a noble horse and he armed him in the best

plate that money could buy and gave him a fine sword. It was arranged that the two knights should fight upon an island, so Sir Tristram sent aboard a ship his horse and all his gear, and departed and landed at the place. His faithful man, Gouvernail, armed him, and then Sir Tristram sent him back on board and himself pricked across the island to where Sir Marhaus was riding his horse up and down.

"Young knight, Sir Tristram, what are you doing here?" Sir Marhaus asked him. "I am regretting your coming. You are too young and untried. Know that I have met some of the greatest knights of all time. Get back to your ship, I counsel you, and let this matter be."

"Fair knight," said Sir Tristram, "how can I, with honour, depart now? I was made knight for just this purpose and I will deliver Cornwall from her tribute payments and win worship on you!"

Sir Marhaus considered him. "Young, unproved knight," he said seriously. "If you can withstand three strokes such as I give, you will win worship of all men! Defend thee!"

So they laid their spears in rest and came together and both men were struck from the saddle with the force of the encounter, and Sir Marhaus wounded Sir Tristram grievously in the side, a wound which troubled him sore, for the spear-head was poisoned. They fought with their swords right fiercely and here the Cornish knight gained, for he was the younger and better-winded and of heavier build. Sir Tristram gave Sir Marhaus such a mighty blow with his sword that it cut through helm and coif of steel and left a piece of the sword-edge lodged in the bone, so that Sir Marhaus was dazed and knew not what he was doing but gave up the fight. Returning to his ship, he sailed for Ireland.

All the greatest surgeons saw him, but no one could save him, and when he died the Queen, his sister, kept the piece of the sword and wrapped it in silk and laid it in her casket.

Meanwhile Sir Tristram, the victor, was so sorely wounded that he sat down on a little hillock, too weak and cold to move until Gouvernail came to help him. Gouvernail took Sir Tristram on board and they sailed across to the mainland, where the King and the seneschal and much people awaited him.

"Hail, noble knight!" said King Mark, and took Tristram in his arms, but all men noted how white and sick the young man appeared.

"His wound must be seen to at once," said the seneschal.

He and King Mark led Tristram into the castle of Tintagel and laid him in a bed. Even selfish, cowardly King Mark wept when he saw the deep cut he had received.

"He will die in an hour or two," said one of the barons.

But hours grew into days, days into weeks, and soon a month had flown by. Sir Tristram continued to lie there, white and still. The King sent out proclamations that any surgeon, no matter whether man or woman, if he had skill to save life, must come forward at once. Many came; but none could do anything. Then word was brought to King Mark.

"There is a strange little woman at the postern gate, sire, and she says she can heal your nephew."

"What is she like?" asked the King, suspiciously. "So many have peered at him and done no good. I do not want him touched again to no purpose."

"She looks wise, and her face is quiet like moonlight, and she wears a red shawl!"

"Well, tell her to do her best," said King Mark.

So the wise old woman went up to Tristram's bed, examined the wound, and glanced with pity at his white face. Then she came before the Cornish king, where he sat with all his barons.

"Sir Tristram will not be healed of this poison in his blood until he journeys to the land from whence it came!"

"If that is so," said King Mark, "then to Ireland must he go at once, but careful must he be, for I doubt not that his name is not liked there!"

Straightway he began to make all ready, and fitted out a ship. Wan and thin, Sir Tristram was carried aboard, but as soon as the salt tang of the sea-breeze blew on him he started to mend. He lay looking at the blue waves and the frothy manes of the white horses and the shifting sun-shadows on the sails overhead, and a little smile curved his lips.

"Bring me my harp," he said, and when he had it his fingers began to play as in other days, and lonely, haunting tunes echoed out over the creamy wake as the brave little ship drove on. Through the morning mists came the green hills of Ireland and the fairy turrets of a kingly castle that stood there in those far-off times.

"The King and Queen of Ireland are staying there," he was told.

Sir Tristram lay on his bed on the deck, and all manner of sweet tunes came to him suddenly as he gazed on that romantic land. He played and played and men listened. Fisherboats put off and rowed around his ship and people stood and listened in the meadows where the shamrocks grew, and everybody was entranced by his playing. Word came to the King and he sent for him. So they carried Sir Tristram ashore and then up to the castle and there he met King Anguish, a noble-looking old man.

"Who are you?" asked the King.

"I am of the country of Liones and my name is Tramtrist," the youth replied.

"Liones in Cornwall," muttered old King Anguish. "That has an ill-sounding ring to me, for in Cornwall I lost the best knight ever I had!" And he told Sir Tristram all the tale of Sir Marhaus.

"It was a right sad thing for you," said Sir Tristram truthfully, and he wondered what would happen if he told all he knew.

"As for this wound you have taken," said the King, "my daughter is very skilled in all manner of surgery and the laws of herbs and simples. If she cannot heal you then you had better prepare for death, for nothing else awaits you!"

"What is your daughter's name?" Tristram asked wonderingly.

"She is called Isoud the Beautiful, and right so. Here she comes herself!"

"It is a true name," said Tristram, as he lay and looked at her, for never in all his life had he seen so fair a face or met with so noble a lady.

"I am come to see to your wound, brave knight," she said, and she brought sweet ointments that were an antidote to the subtle poison, and she healed him within a few weeks.

Many happy hours they spent together in that tapestried chamber. Sometimes she read him old romances from vellum-bound, hand-written books; sometimes he played to her, and at last he taught her also to play the harp.

Isoud learned to love Tristram very dearly. She wondered much about him and what his history had been in the country of Liones beyond the sea. He too loved her for her great kindness, but it was not in the same way as she loved him.

CHAPTER 15

SIR TRISTRAM JOUSTS FOR A LADY

THERE was at that time at the court of the Irish king a noble knight, a Saracen, and he was called Sir Palamides. He loved Isoud the Beautiful and would fain wed with her, but she did not return his love. He brought her wonderful presents each day, perfumed silks from India and sandalwood trinket-boxes and fair gems from Persia. Tristram saw all this and was sorry for Isoud, for she could not be rid of Sir Palamides; but there was nothing he could do for her at that time.

Then King Anguish announced a great joust and tournament. Heralds carried the news of it to England, Wales, Scotland, France and Brittany. Soon, famous knights began landing in Ireland with their arms and their horses, so that the flower of chivalry was assembled at King Anguish's court. Isoud came to Tristram and her beautiful face was dark with worry.

"Oh, Tramtrist, will you help me?" she said. And she told him of the tournament and that she feared Sir Palamides would be proclaimed the winner and claim her as his prize.

"I owe you my life," he answered simply, "but I am a poor knight compared with these great names. What is it that I can do?" He looked at her gratefully. "I fear I am not fit to joust."

"But I am so unhappy," mourned Isoud. "Sir Palamides is a mighty knight and likely to win over all others and then he will ask for my hand as the victor and there will be then no help for me."

"He may very well win," mused Tristram, "for he is a proved knight and I but young and lately made one. At my first encounter, as I have told you, I was nearly slain. But, for all that,

I will be there and I will do my best to save you—only tell no one of my intention lest they try to stop me."

"I will not tell," Isoud promised, her face alight with joy. "I will get you horse and harness and all you need!"

On the great day, Sir Palamides rode out resplendent in gold inlaid plate, white plumes and a black shield. His horse was in trappings of black-and-gold and a gold cloth covered its back. The people cheered to see him, for he was a passing fair sight.

Many of King Arthur's knights were there and many from France and Scotland. When the jousting began, Sir Palamides soon showed of what metal he was made, for he was almost invincible. Down into the dust before his lance went Sir Gawaine and Sir Gaheris; Sir Agravaine and King Bagdemagus fared no better.

Sir Palamides waited for more knights to come out to meet him, and his fine, bronze, hawk-like face was proud as he glanced across to the stands where among the fair ladies was Isoud the Beautiful. Sir Kay next rode out, but Sir Kay also went crashing into the dust and so did Sir Sagramore and many others. So on that first day Sir Palamides won much honour.

On the second day it looked again as if the Saracen was going to overthrow all contestants; but Isoud had managed to get horse and armour by this time, all in pure silver-white. With her own fair hands she armed her knight, buckling and strapping the heavy suit upon him.

"Quick now, out of the castle by this private postern," she whispered. "Your horse is ready there. Ride now quickly to the lists ere Sir Palamides has unhorsed all the brave men who meet him today!"

When the people saw Sir Tristram riding into the field all in silver-white they cried aloud, so bright and glorious did he look. Sir Palamides saw him and laid spear in rest, and the two galloped to meet one another. Then all the people began shouting and crying out, for, lo, Sir Tristram was galloping on down the field, and there lay Sir Palamides groaning on the ground.

Isoud was so glad and thankful that her eyes sparkled and shone. Sir Tristram rode to the centre of the field and waited quietly—a new lance in his hand, his aspect undismayed. Sir

Palamides had picked himself up and crept away, for his heart was sore with shame.

"Will no one joust with the white knight?" the heralds cried.

But no one would come forward to essay so formidable a knight. So Sir Tristram whirled his horse about and galloped after Sir Palamides and overtook him and forced him to promise that he would woo the Lady Isoud no more, nor bear arms again for a twelve-month, and Sir Palamides had to consent there in the meadows in sore distress and humiliation. He doffed his armour and threw it down and went away grieving.

The King and all the court soon discovered who it was who had won at the jousts, and Sir Tristram was more honoured than before. But it came about that on the day after he was taking a hot bath, his squires attending him. The Queen and Isoud were waiting in his outer chamber until he should be ready to go riding with them. The Queen touched Sir Tristram's harness and shield and examined his blazon and the embroidery of his coat with the deep interest of a woman to whom knightly arms and all heraldry were an open book. To Isoud the Beautiful they were the arms and harness of a hero, and her heart glowed.

"There is his sword," said the Queen, for it lay upon the silk cover of the bed where he had thrown it. "Fain would I look at so noble a blade!"

She drew it out of its sheath and the steel glittered balefully. But not for that reason did her speech die on her tongue or her face whiten as if she had been struck by death. Eighteen inches from the point was a place on the blade where a piece of steel had been broken off and was missing.

"Alas, fair lady mother, why do you look so?" said Isoud.

"The traitor knight that slew my brother!" cried the Queen. "He was this Sir Tramtrist, who is here in this castle! Yet must we make sure and doubly sure, for honour's sake!"

To her chamber she went and to her casket, where long months ago she had hidden the sliver of steel taken from Sir Marhaus's wound after his death. Then back she came, ashen of face and nigh to fainting, and fitted the piece into the sword. The two fell together so perfectly that no man could have said where was the crack.

In a rage of grief she grasped the weapon and ran and would have stabbed Sir Tristram in his bath if his men had not held her and taken away the sword. Foiled in this purpose, she ran sobbing to the King and told him all.

He was shocked, but he tried to comfort her, though his heart was heavy.

"Leave it," he said. "I will deal with this matter, sad though it is, for better knight I never knew."

He went to his guest and straightly asked for an explanation, and as straightly Tristram told him all—how he had taken on the fight with Sir Marhaus for his uncle the King's sake, who could find no champion.

"What I did was for my country and I did only what you would have done in my place, sire," he said fearlessly. "I had to seek this fair land of yours for healing and so I let change my name!"

The King nodded slowly. "You did as a knight should, and I cannot blame you," he said heavily. "But now you must leave us, for my barons and my Queen will not let you remain here after this."

"I will go," Sir Tristram replied, "but I pray you let me take leave of your daughter and of all your knights, and go openly and unafraid, not as a dog, sneaking away."

"That is granted," agreed the King.

Then Sir Tristram thanked him for all his kindness and hospitality, and went to Isoud the Beautiful to say farewell. She wept sore at his departing, and told him that she would never marry unless with his consent and that he should be the one to find her a husband, though in her heart she hoped it would be himself. So they exchanged rings as tokens of remembrance, and he left her there lamenting.

Down into the great echoing hall he went, where all the knights and barons were assembled, and he faced them all proudly.

"Before I leave you," he said aloud, "I would ask this of you all—if any of you have any cause to be displeased with me or in any way feel I have wronged you, speak and come forward and I will give honourable satisfaction in battle; say nothing behind my back, but speak out here before me, and we will settle it once for all!"

He stood there waiting in a silence so great that the fluttering of a bat's wing in the lofty raftered roof came sharply distinct. The sunlight fell through the stone window slits and shone upon him. But no one stirred and no one spoke. There were men there who were of the Queen's kin and Sir Marhaus's kin, but they held their peace, and so he turned on his heel and departed and took ship to Cornwall.

CHAPTER 16

THE SORROWFUL KNIGHT

As TIME went on, King Mark became very jealous of Sir Tristram and sought for some means of killing him, for the Cornish king was a cowardly man and hated the shining splendour of Sir Tristram's knighthood. He kept his feelings hidden as much as he might.

Sir Tristram had told him of all his adventures in Ireland, and described to him Lady Isoud the Beautiful.

"Fain would I wed her," said King Mark, "for I have no Queen and it is meet and fitting that there should be a lovely lady reigning over the fair Cornish lands. Sir Tristram, I give to you the noble task of sailing to Ireland and bringing my bride to me!"

He thought in his wicked heart that it was quite possible that Sir Tristram would never return.

"I will well," Sir Tristram answered, for he thought that it would be wonderful for the lady to be a queen and it pleased him to think that he could have a hand in it as a small return for her love and kindness to him. He did not dream how dearly she loved him, Tristram, and how she would have journeyed the world to be beside him.

So he set sail with Cornish knights, all arrayed in the finest clothes and with horses and arms. Weatherwise sailors shook their heads when Sir Tristram went aboard, for he knew nothing of the sea and its ways, and gave command to loose the sails when a strange golden light brooded on the sea and things distant seemed near. Low black clouds lay in thick banks upon the sea, and the wind was moaning uneasily. Bravely enough the ship heeled over to the push of the wind and sea, and the waves ran hissing along her sides, but darker and thicker grew the tempest, and the ship was driven before it as a chip of wood is swirled down a stream. For days the storm raged, and when at last it had blown itself out the little ship was so damaged that it had to limp into a cove with its sails torn and split.

"This is a fair green land," said Sir Tristram, gazing at the rich forests, battlemented castles and silver rivers. "What name has it?"

"This is King Arthur's country," he was told, "and hard by is Camelot!"

So he went ashore, wondering greatly at the chance which had brought him here. He set up his pavilion and hung his shield upon it to see if by any chance a passing knight would give him the pleasure of jousting with him.

Presently across the daisied meadowland rode two knights, Sir Ector de Maris and Sir Morganor, and they saw the stranger's shield with its unfamiliar blazon and so they touched it with their spears as a signal that they would have ado with the knight who owned it.

Sir Tristram donned his armour while they sat their horses and tarried for him and argued what knight this might be. Presently he rode out, and first he unhorsed Sir Ector and then Sir Morganor, both with one spear, which did not splinter. As they lay on the ground, fetching their breath, they marvelled greatly at his strength.

"Who are you and of what country?" asked Sir Ector de Maris.

"My name is Sir Tristram," he told them, "and I come from Cornwall."

"Now woe is me," cried Sir Ector in disgust. "Never thought I to be overcome by a Cornishman!"

And he was so passing angry about it that he took off his armour and walked back to his castle, for he would not ride. Sir Tristram smiled at his conceit and went back to his pavilion. There came to him his faithful man, Gouvernail.

"Wist ye that King Anguish of Ireland is here in Camelot on a charge of killing one of the cousins of Sir Bleoberis de Ganis and Sir Blamore de Ganis when this cousin was in Ireland?"

In those days a knight could be thus summoned for treason, as it was called, and must answer the summons and either give satisfaction to the accusing party by fighting himself or appointing a champion to do it for him. The good old man had answered the summons in a knightly fashion and travelled to Camelot with all haste.

King Arthur was absent, but he appointed King Carados and the King of the Scots to act in his place as judges.

"Ah," said Sir Tristram joyously, "now have I a chance to help that good knight and king who showed me so much good grace at his court. Lead me to him, Gouvernail, for I will take over this battle for him."

So Gouvernail told the King that Tristram of Liones would have speech with him and right so came Sir Tristram. He would have held the King's horse for him, but he dismounted and took him in his arms.

"Oh, my boy, my boy, never had I such need of a good friend and noble knight," said the old King. "I am summoned for the death, in my country, of a knight that was kin unto Sir Launcelot. I am to fight Sir Blamore de Ganis. Now, all these knights of King Ban's blood, Sir Launcelot and the others, are among the hardiest knights there are, and mighty fighters!"

"Nathless will I do this battle for you," said Sir Tristram; "only first tell me and swear to me that you are in the right and had no hand in the killing."

The King assured him that it was so.

"Well, then," answered Tristram, "let them know that your champion is ready!"

So King Anguish went to the judges and told them he had found one who would fight for him, and right so Sir Tristram marched into the hall and stood looking at them all with his level glance that had the fire of steel in it. And many there clutched their weapons and shuffled together and spoke in whispers.

"It is Sir Tristram, the knight who killed Sir Marhaus," one said.

"It is Sir Tristram, the only knight who unhorsed Sir Palamides at the jousts," cried another.

But he was accepted, and preparations went forward for the combat.

Sir Bleoberis went to his brother, Sir Blamore. "Dear brother, I have no need to remind you," he said seriously, "we are of Launcelot's kin, and no man of our family was ever shamed. This Sir Tristram is as steel and lightning, men say, therefore should he overcome you choose death rather than yield!"

"Do not doubt me," answered Sir Blamore. "If by his great prowess he smites me down he will have to slay me, for I will not yield to him and he will have no choice in the matter, as he is deciding the issue by combat!"

Into the lists rode the two men on the day appointed. The judges leaned forward to see, and all the knights whispered and marvelled among themselves. Down went the lances into rest and the horses were urged forward so as to meet with as great a shock as possible.

With a thunderous crash the two knights came together, and Sir Blamore and his horse went down in a smother of white dust. But he was up in an instant.

"Alight, Sir Tristram, and continue the fight," he shouted, "for though my horse has failed me the good earth will not."

So they came together with swords and fought like madmen, and such was the speed and dash of that encounter that those watching marvelled only that the men had time to breathe. Then, with a terrible blow on his helm, Sir Blamore was down, and this time he fell on his side and was too weak to rise.

With sword drawn, Sir Tristram stood over him and stared down at him. In his heart he was sore troubled, for Sir Blamore had not cried for mercy.

But if he was uncertain what to do, Sir Blamore was not. "Fair knight," he said, in a weak but steady voice, "slay me now, and quickly. I will die now with worship, not live with shame!"

At these knightly words, Sir Tristram was perplexed and did not know what to do. He did not want to kill him, for Sir Launcelot's sake, but he had little choice. Unless Sir Blamore yielded, he must kill him, for he was championing another.

"Yield thee," he whispered, but the other man gazed on him in quiet courage, and would not.

Then did Sir Tristram walk slowly right across the lists to the judges' stand and there he kneeled him down.

"My lords, kings and gentlemen," he cried in a loud clear voice, "for King Arthur's and Sir Launcelot's sake, take this matter into your own hands! It were shame and pity to slay so noble a man; but, as you have heard, he refuses mercy. King Anguish, as I fight for you and am your true champion, pray speak for him."

"I wish him no harm," said the King of Ireland. "Judges decide you for us!"

"Call Sir Bleoberis, his brother," said King Carados.

Proudly and coldly answered Sir Bleoberis: "Sir Tristram has beaten his body, but never his spirit. Let him finish the matter and slay him!"

"No, it shall not be!" said all the judges.

Sir Bleoberis bowed his head in assent to their final word, rejoicing in his heart that his brother should live with honour.

"Bring them together," ordered King Carados, so Sir Tristram, Sir Blamore, Sir Bleoberis and King Anguish greeted one another and made there a friendship to last their lives. And because of his gentle chivalry in this memorable battle, Sir Tristram was beloved by all the blood of Sir Launcelot for ever.

Then Sir Tristram and the King set sail for Ireland and they were received there with gladness, even the Queen welcoming Sir Tristram for the sake of her husband. It was a happy and joyful time, very different from when he had been there before; but Isoud the Beautiful was the happiest of all to see her hero again, for she loved him dearly.

Then came King Anguish to Sir Tristram. "What shall I do for you, good knight?" he asked, gazing with pride and joy at the champion who had freed him so that he had been able to return to his own people.

Sir Tristram remembered his mission and asked for the hand of Isoud the Beautiful for his uncle. King Anguish's face fell and he sighed.

"It shall be as you say, but, oh, Tristram, I had so wanted to call you in truth my son. I had hoped you would wed her yourself."

"If I did that," Tristram answered gently, "I should break a promise and become a false knight indeed. I pray that you will do this thing for me!"

"I will," said King Anguish, and he went away sorrowfully to make preparations.

Isoud the Beautiful was told, and her heart was sad that she should never wed Sir Tristram. She wondered what Cornwall would be like and how she should feel as a queen. Little she knew of the sad cloud that hung over the man she loved. For the Queen, who was sore troubled in her mind, seeing her daughter loving and not being loved in return, said to Dame Bragwaine, her woman, "I place in your charge this subtly brewed poison. When you are at the Cornish court, see to it that King Mark and my daughter drink to each other in this strange fairy wine and they shall love one another truly and devotedly till death, and Isoud will be spared suffering on account of the good knight, Sir Tristram."

Dame Bragwaine promised to deal faithfully in the matter, and she hid the flask in the cabin of the ship. In all the bravery of fine clothes, Sir Tristram and Isoud embarked for the shores of Cornwall. As the ship headed out into the blue of the deep sea, he led her down to the great cabin to rest her.

"This sea air makes me thirst," she said.

"Here is a flask hidden," said Sir Tristram. "I wot that your woman and my man have kept this for themselves; but it seems a rare and good wine!"

He took a golden cup and filled it and they drank one to the other, laughing and gay as children. The wine ran down as fire and their heads swam, and suddenly in each other's eyes they were all the world and all the love and beauty of it! And for the rest of their lives that love never left them, and because of it Sir Tristram suffered the cruellest torture a man may, for he kept his word as a knight should and took Isoud the Beautiful to

D

Cornwall to his uncle. She was in his heart by day and in his dreams by night; life became without savour to him and his heart was near to breaking; but still he held to his word and she was married to King Mark.

The King soon guessed that Isoud's heart was not his and never would be, for Tristram had it and she his, and so his hate became blacker and blacker against the man who had served him faithfully at all times and in all things.

And all this is the reason why men said and still say that Sir Tristram lived to be true to his name, which means "born in sorrow".

CHAPTER 17

THE COWARD KNIGHT

THE more King Mark heard about Sir Tristram and his deeds the more he hated him. He banished him from the lands of Cornwall, and so Tristram went to England, where he had many strange adventures. Whenever a messenger came to the Cornish court or a minstrel sang sweet lays to Queen Isoud, Sir Tristram's name was always to the fore. His mighty deeds were set down and written as ballads, and all people heard them.

"He is my own nephew," King Mark said savagely, "but I loathe his very name. Evil has he done me, for I have not the love of my Queen. He has it all that is traitor to me. I will send some of my own chosen men, who will watch and bring word to me if he really is as great as men say, for happen much that we hear is rumour!"

"I also will send men of mine," the Queen whispered to herself, "and I shall know the truth!"

Weeks passed, and then, one by one, the messengers made their way back and they swore to the truth of their words. No man except Sir Launcelot could withstand Sir Tristram, for each knight he met at jousting he unhorsed, and if he were an evil knight he was slain.

King Mark went into his chamber and slammed the door, for he was black with rage. If any had crossed him that day, it would have fared ill with him.

Queen Isoud laughed and danced with pleasure at what she heard of Sir Tristram. Presently she heard a mighty shouting and commotion and there was a noise of pages running and the jar and slam of coffer lids.

"What is toward?" she asked.

"The King has sent for raiment and is disguising himself for a journey into England," she was told. "He means to seek out Sir Tristram and slay him."

"What men are they that go with him?" asked Isoud.

"Sir Bersules and Sir Amant."

"They are good men," the Queen said slowly, and she went to the turret window and looked out over the waving green woods; her eyes were swimming with tears.

King Mark journeyed to England, and there he and his knights rode many miles through the pleasant country where summer ferns and field-lilies grew and shy deer grazed and gazed.

"It is a very long way we go," growled King Mark. "There is a horseman coming. We will speak to him touching this matter. Ho, there, fair sir, where is King Arthur?"

"Even at Camelot, noble knight," the horseman made answer, and he looked amazed that anyone should not know this, but he supposed that they were from a foreign land.

"Hast heard anything of a knight at Camelot called Sir Tristram?" went on King Mark, hoping in his black heart to hear ill tidings.

"Yes, yes, indeed!" said the other knight, his tone enthusiastic. "Sir Tristram is at Camelot and no man of such worship has been there this many a long day. At his last battle he fought with Sir Launcelot and that was indeed a great fight. The two were so well matched that neither could gain the advantage, but each yielded the degree to the other. King Arthur has made him a knight of the Round Table. The siege of the good knight Sir Marhaus was not filled and they put him there!"

The horseman rode on and King Mark sat gloomily biting his lips and scowling. "Look you," he said to his two knights as they rode on again, "this is what I plan to do. I trust you two the most of all my men. Know then that I came over here for one reason only and that is to kill Sir Tristram and clear my path of him for ever. As he is such a worshipful fighter we shall have to catch him with wiles and treason and so destroy him utterly."

The two men stared at him aghast, and Sir Bersules's face was dark with anger and scorn.

"This is a shameful thing, sire," he cried. "Had I known that you meant this, I had never ridden here with you! And I will no farther go but leave you here, for I will never sully my honour so by planning murder against a good man!"

The King whirled on him, so blinded by his rage that he appeared out of his mind. "Traitor knight!" he screamed, and drew his sword.

Sir Bersules had no time to defend himself, but as he saw his death coming a look of high scorn flashed from his eyes. For greater coolness he was riding with his helm at his saddlebow, and King Mark's sword took him across the brow and killed him on the instant.

Sir Amant and the squires cried out in horror.

"Ah, shameful deed! Oh, most unknightly deed!" cried Sir Amant. "We also will leave you and will accuse you of treason before King Arthur!"

"No, that shall you never," cried King Mark, and he kicked his spurs into his horse's sides so that it leaped forward upon the men. His sword was raised to strike them down, but they stood together and laughed at his evil malice. He was forced to rein in his horse, for he was afraid of attempting more than one at a time. So he whirled about and rode away, leaving them to bury the body of the valiant Sir Bersules. For a long distance the King trotted his horse through the woods. At length he came to a fountain, and there he saw a knight sitting brooding, his countenance rueful, as it well might be. He kept muttering and sighing unhappily for the love of a lady who was not for him. Plainly, his heart was heavy.

"Fair knight, this is a piteous complaint," said King Mark.

The other turned to stare at him. "It is a thousand times worse than you can imagine," he said shortly.

"What is your name?" asked the King.

"Sir Lamorak de Galis. By your speech you should be from Cornwall. That is where the cowardly King Mark reigns, the wickedest knight in all Christendom. 'Tis shame that so mean a man should have so fair a lady as Isoud the Beautiful."

"Of this I know nothing," lied the King, dismayed at hearing such evil things of himself. "Are there any tidings from Camelot?" he went on quickly.

"There is to be a tournament at the Castle of Jagent, near there. All the foremost knights will be there. Ha, here comes a friend of mine, Sir Dinadan! Sir Dinadan, this is a Cornish knight travelling in these parts."

Sir Dinadan gave a slight sneer. "I suppose he could not longer live within the realm of the cowardly tyrant King Mark. Come, Cornish Knight, and joust with me!"

"No, no, that will I not," said the King hastily, for he misliked the big, burly-looking Sir Dinadan, and his flesh crept as he surveyed his mighty lance.

"Well, if you will not joust with me," said Sir Dinadan with a bantering laugh, "why not run a course with Sir Lamorak here?"

"If I must," said King Mark sulkily.

So they two rode together, spears in rest. Sir Lamorak's spear caught in a chink of the King's armour, and the Cornishman was carried over his horse's tail like an apple on a bodkin, ere he dropped off. The two men rode on, leaving him there, and they were laughing openly. Even a coward like King Mark could be goaded into battle, and he was now so furious that he mounted and thundered after them.

"What now?" asked Sir Lamorak.

"Fight me with a sword," said the King thickly, "for I will not be so shamed!" And he flew at Sir Lamorak so that he must draw and defend himself.

Sir Lamorak tried not to do the King any real hurt, for there was something rather pitiful in his cowardly vexation. But King Mark was so angry and lashed about him so furiously that, perforce, Sir Lamorak had to exert himself. He gave his adversary a mighty blow on the helm so that he wilted in his saddle and hung his head.

"What cheer now?" asked Sir Lamorak, in some concern. "You look to have had your fill of fighting!"

"We are ill-matched," growled the King.

"*You* could not match up to a good knight," sneered Sir Dinadad. "Come, let us ride on. I do suppose we had better conduct this mean knight on his way with us lest evil befall him."

It was not so long before the three came to a bridge with a tower at the end of it and there was a well-armed man on horse-back, proffering himself to joust.

"Here is a right noble chance for you, stranger knight," said Sir Dinadan. "Offer yourself for a spear-running with him!"

King Mark was too ashamed to refuse, so he laid his spear in rest and galloped forward to the encounter. He and the other knight each broke his spear on his opponent's shield, but both men remained in the saddle.

"Here is another spear for you," said the knight of the bridge, offering a new ash pole to King Mark. "We will joust further if you will?"

"No, I shall not," King Mark replied shortly. "You can keep your spear. Fellows, let us ride on to yonder castle and try and get hospitality for the night. Who owns it?"

"It is Sir Tor's castle," said Sir Dinadan, "but the lieutenant of the castle is a worshipful knight who will not refuse us."

So they were made welcome and supped and had good cheer and then into the big central hall where they sat came their host, Sir Berluse, to see that they had all they wanted. Then his genial smile vanished, and stern disapproval burned in his dark eyes.

"King Mark!" he cried aloud, and his voice rang upon the metal shields on the walls. "I know you better than you know me. You it is who slew my father. For the love of Sir Tor and Sir Lamorak, I will not hurt you or your company in this castle, but once you are off my ground I warn you I shall hunt you to the death. You are not fit to be in the company of these good knights, for you are a black-hearted traitor."

King Mark was so stunned and ashamed at this attack that words failed him. But Sir Lamorak and Sir Dinadan were as much astounded, for, had they known who he was, they would not have ridden one yard in his company.

Next day, Sir Dinadan and King Mark set off early. Having promised to conduct the King to Camelot, Sir Dinadan had perforce to keep his word and stay with him. Soon after them came Sir Berluse, and with him two of his cousins, to do battle.

"I'm sorry from my heart, Dinadan, that you are on his side," Sir Berluse cried out, "but I suppose you must keep by him, so now do your best!"

They came together, and, as he had support, King Mark really exerted himself. Because Sir Dinadan was a truly wonderful fighter the combat was soon over, for Sir Berluse was down and his cousins discomforted. Sir Dinadan had just ridden against one of them, but turning swiftly he was in time to see King Mark about to butcher Sir Berluse where he lay helpless in the heather. Speechless with disgust, he dismounted and dragged the King, snarling, away from the wounded man.

"You are nothing but a common murderer," he said. "Mount and ride, before I forget my knighthood and kick you as you deserve."

So they rode, and they had many adventures by the way, but at last they came to a thin wood where there was an old well. Sitting about on the grass eating their noon meat were six knights-errant; their horses were near at hand cropping the grass. Sir Dinadan smiled slyly to himself.

"Now, King Mark," he thought, "now shall we have some merry sport! Come," he went on aloud, "let us essay these bold knights and win worship!"

"What?" cried the King, in horror. "Now heaven forbid, for they are six and we are two."

"The more honour, brother," said Sir Dinadan and laid his spear in rest and galloped forward, expecting King Mark to follow suit.

And so he did—but in the opposite direction and as fast as he could go!

When Sir Dinadan saw that he raised his spear out of rest, slung his shield round upon his back again, and, laughing mightily, rode forward to join the band, who were all King Arthur's knights. Right gladly was he welcomed.

CHAPTER 18

THE RUNAWAY

SIR DINADAN had promised King Mark that he would not spread abroad who he was nor tell his name. So, when the six knights-errant talked with him as they sat and dined all together under the trees in their wood, he kept silent about the coward knight.

"What knight was that who so suddenly left you and galloped away?" one of them asked.

"He," said Sir Dinadan, with a harsh laugh, "was a knight from Cornwall, the most fearful coward ever I saw, for when he realised that there were six of you his heart misgave him. Where are you thinking of spending the night?"

"There is a castle in the valley yonder where dwells an old knight. He has fought in many wars and battles and dearly loves all knights-errant and welcomes them, so that he and they may sit by the blazing logs and tell tales far into the night. We will go there!"

When they arrived, Sir Dinadan, who had not been there before, was greatly pleased with the lichened grey walls and soaring turrets, which seemed to touch the stars. So he left the others and walked round the fortalice. A white face at one of the windows was watching him covertly, and he glanced at it and thought he should know its features.

"Ho, my runaway knight, King Mark!" he said. "Why did you fly so sudden? Had you no stomach for a fight?"

"Sir Dinadan," said the King, "I did not dare to stay, for there were so many against us, and I marvel greatly to see you alive at this time. When I left you I thought that you were foolishly galloping to your death! You must be a mighty man of valour to have so escaped. Fair sir, tell me, are they all dead?"

"No, they are not dead," Sir Dinadan answered coldly. "They were, as I found, my friends, and such are safe from me! It is only coward enemies whom I hate!" And he looked sternly at the King.

But King Mark took no notice of the rebuke. "Who was their leader?" he asked.

Exasperated by the shallow fears and conceits of the fellow, Sir Dinadan thought to give him a fright. "Sir Launcelot is their captain," he said, watching the other's expression.

King Mark began to fidget and shake at his window. "Prithee, tell me how I may know Sir Launcelot," he urged, "that I may avoid him."

"You will know him if ever you meet him," said Sir Dinadan; "he, and he only, has a shield of silver and black bends!"

Now, this device was the one that Sir Mordred bore and not Sir Launcelot, for Sir Launcelot was not in that band of knights-errant at all; but Sir Dinadan had gained his point, for King Mark was terrified now. Sir Dinadan left him and went back to his friends, among whom was Sir Griflet and Sir Mordred. They fell to talking of the Cornish knight and Sir Dinadan told them that he was lodging in the same castle as they were.

"I have a notion," said Sir Griflet, "for here with us is Sir Dagonet, King Arthur's fool. He is the best and merriest knight who ever couched lance or made the King to laugh at tourney and joust. What say you, Sir Dagonet? Wilt help us to teach a mean knight better ways?"

"I will well," said the merry little man. "What is in your mind?"

Sir Dinadan and Sir Giflet both began to laugh. "I told the Cornish knight," said Sir Dinadan, "that Sir Launcelot was one of you and was here leading you. He asked me what his shield was and I described Sir Mordred's. Now do you see what I am thinking of and what Sir Griflet is thinking of too, though he knew not about the shield?"

"Yes," Sir Mordred grunted, smiling into his beard. "I am not yet well of my hurts and cannot ride nor bear my harness upon my back as yet. Borrow my gear and let Sir Dagonet wear it and have a right merry jest hunting the Cornishman about! And if he thinks—as he must—that it is Sir Launcelot who is after him, well, the very birds of chase and woodland are like to laugh!"

"That which suits you, suits me," said the jester, with a merry grin.

So they armed him next day and set him on a horse and gave him shield and spear and all together they rode to a place where they knew that King Mark would pass, and there they waited.

"We will hide in this leafy brake and enjoy what sport is to be seen," said Sir Griflet. "Now hark; I hear already the drumming of horse's hooves. Lo, here comes he! Ride forth, brave Sir Dagonet!"

So the court jester spurred his horse out upon the woodland way, and there he waited till he could see that it was indeed King Mark. Then he galloped to meet him.

"Defend thee, sir knight, for I am coming to slay thee," he shouted.

King Mark took one look at the dread shield of Sir Launcelot's.

"It is he, it is the matchless knight himself," he sobbed, a stranglehold of terror upon his throat.

Right so, he wheeled his horse and thundered off as hard as he could go through bush and undergrowth, splashing over streams and hurtling through hedges. After him galloped Sir Dagonet, yelling to him to turn and fight. The shock of the chase could be heard a mile away. The rooks flew up startled from the elms of the forest as the knight and his pursuer thundered below. Sir Dinadan, Sir Mordred, Sir Griflet and the others stood and held their sides and laughed until they were spent for breath.

At last Sir Dinadan said: "We must ride and see what is toward. No harm must come to Sir Dagonet, for King Arthur loves him and made him knight with his own hands. Follow we at once!"

So they rode along, spreading out among the trees, calling to Sir Dagonet. Far, far ahead of them, King Mark raced along. As he galloped, he espied in front of him an armed knight who was loitering about on his horse hoping for some knight-errant to pass that way and have some spear-running with him. When he heard King Mark's horse, he looked up eagerly and was amazed at sight of an armed knight flying from combat.

"Fie and for shame!" he shouted. "Stand and do battle worshipfully. See, I will be on your side and fight with you as a brother!"

"Let me pass, let me pass," King Mark cried. "Behind me

comes the best knight in all the world, and I trow it is no shame to fly from him, for death is all I get if I tarry. Behold the black-bended shield!"

"Still I say fie!" said the other stoutly. "If it is Sir Launcelot or Sir Tristram, still will I essay them. Come, I will have no argument. Stand and fight!"

King Mark reined in then, for this man seemed a very bold and likely fighter and he himself was nearly spent with the chase. Perhaps, after all, it were better to turn against the foe now that he was to have help.

They soon espied Sir Dagonet as he came riding swiftly down the forest glades. The stranger knight spurred to meet him, and his spear caught Sir Dagonet, unhorsing him as easily as a ripe acorn leaps from its cup.

"You have broken his neck," said King Mark admiringly, but the knight shrugged.

"No, he is alive," he said. "Here comes another of them."

Sir Brandiles was ahead of the others, and when he saw the jester's terrible fall he knew the jest was no longer merry.

"Defend yourself," he cried angrily and rode hard against the strange knight.

They hurtled together and Sir Bradiles went down before the other's lance. Sir Uwaine was the next, and down he went also, and Sir Ozana.

"Hold a moment, before we do more against him," suggested Sir Griflet. "Ho, squires, ride across to him and find out who he is and if he belongs to King Arthur's court. He fights as hardily as if he were Sir Launcelot!"

"My name, ha! They seek to know what I shall not tell," the knight answered fiercely. "This only you may tell them. I am not of King Arthur's court. Now let them come on and fight, not stand prating there like old crones over a hedge."

"This man is a very worthy knight," said Sir Agravaine, one of the party. "He has overthrown three of us, and we shall all have to try him for very shame. I will run against him first!"

He tucked his arm about his spear as strongly as he could and gripped his horse with his knees to see if it were not possible to avoid a fall. But, alas, he fared no better; nor did the others.

There were left only Sir Dinadan, who had not yet come up with them, and Sir Mordred, who was unarmed.

So the strange knight waited a moment or two more and then rode away, King Mark at his elbow loud in praise of him. One of the King's varlets had found out who this mighty fighter was and came and whispered to his master.

"Sir, it is Sir Palamides, the great Saracen knight," he told him, and King Mark was well pleased that such a worthy man had rescued him, as he thought, from Sir Launcelot. They parted after resting awhile, and Sir Palamides rode off into the forest.

At long last King Mark reached King Arthur's court. There was a great stir there as if something of import had occurred and he wondered uneasily what it might be. He was soon told.

"There is a knight here that has accused you of treason before King Arthur. He did not give your name, but the description of your armour tallies. Will you come before the King?"

"Yes, I will come," muttered King Mark. He knew that it must be Sir Amant, who, true to a promise he had given after the slaying of Sir Bersules, had not revealed that the slayer was the King of Cornwall.

"Is this accusation true that you slew his friend?" King Arthur asked.

And, coward though he was, King Mark dared not deny it. "It is true," he growled.

"Then must you fight that he may have satisfaction," the King said seriously. "Go to the lists and settle it, for it is ill waiting on these things."

They departed and fought and, as ill adventure would have it, King Mark's spear wounded Sir Amant in the side so that he had only an hour or two to live. Even King Mark was troubled, and he thought to escape from the place before knights who knew him should, perchance, return. He mounted and galloped away from Camelot as fast as he could go.

There were three maidens at court who had been with Isoud the Beautiful. They knew Sir Amant and went in haste to attend him, weeping sore for him.

"There is nothing you can do," he said weakly. "I am killed in a righteous quarrel, for that man slew Sir Bersules and now me, for that we would not plot to kill Sir Tristram. Tell Sir Tristram I died for him, but pity me not. Rather would I die for him than live for myself!"

Then they knew that the slayer was none other than King Mark, and they went to King Arthur and told him all. In all the time that he had reigned at Camelot he had never shown such anger, and so wrathful were all the knights assembled there that had the Cornishman been present he might have died from fear.

When Sir Tristram heard the tale, he sat down in the window and took his head in his hands and wept sore for his friends, for he had known and loved both Sir Bersules and Sir Amant. Deep sobs shook him. Sir Launcelot saw him thus and mourned at his friend's woe.

"King Arthur," he begged, "let me go after that false knight!"

"You shall," agreed the King, "but, Launcelot, harken to me —slay him not. No honour will come to any who spears such as he!"

Launcelot waited for no more, but, grieving for Sir Tristram, armed himself quickly and rode after the Cornishman. Three miles he galloped without drawing rein, and then he saw before him the figure of the man he wanted.

"Turn!" shouted Sir Launcelot in a mighty voice. "Turn, King Mark, for I have come to take you to King Arthur's court, if you like it or if you like it not! Turn and face me, coward."

"Who is it speaks," asked King Mark nervously.

"Sir Launcelot, so defend you, for I am coming for you!" And Sir Launcelot spurred his horse and charged down on the cowering knight.

"Stop, stop! I yield me to you, Sir Launcelot, great and worthy sir," cried the King in terror.

But Sir Launcelot, pretending not to hear him, thundered on.

"I am lost!" moaned the King. "I will no defence make, for he can hardly slay me unresisting if he is such a man of worship as they say!"

He did not so much dismount as fall from his horse, and from the ground he cried for mercy.

Sir Launcelot reined in and sat his horse, gazing down on the recumbent figure, disgust and scorn on his face.

"Get up, recreant knight," he cried.

"I will not fight; I tell you I will not fight," King Mark answered. "But I will go with you where you will."

"I wish," said Sir Launcelot, between his teeth, "I wish that I could have given you just one buffet. It would have eased me much!" He sighed. "Get up, craven, and mount your horse."

And so he brought him to King Arthur's court. "He is here, sire," he said, and when Mark saw King Arthur he tore off his helm and threw it away, drew his sword and flung it after the helm, and then fell down flat on his face, beseeching grace and mercy.

King Arthur rubbed his chin and mused as he looked down on him. "I am glad to see you there, Mark, and yet I am not glad," he said. "You should make amends for the evil you have done. You should have sworn fealty to me, and that you never would do. You have killed good knights and done wrong to me. What have you to say?"

"I will make amends," King Mark promised eagerly, for he was a soft-tongued rogue. "I would fain be in accord with Sir Tristram and let all this unhappy matter be over between us!"

"I wonder if I may trust you?" said King Arthur.

But he loved Sir Tristram dearly, and he hoped, in his generous way, that King Mark meant what he said. So he brought them together and heard King Mark tell Sir Tristram what he had told him. But King Mark spoke with his tongue only; his heart was not in his words; but no man knew this. Even Sir Tristram, who had such cause to mistrust him, believed that he was sincere; so, knightly, he made accord with him.

CHAPTER 19

BREUNOR AND THE LION

A YOUNG man walked into the courtyard of King Arthur's castle one autumn afternoon when the knights were at play or practice.

King Arthur looked on him and smiled, for ever he loved to see a well-made man, and this one was strong and tall. His coat was of cloth-of-gold, but it hung badly upon him and made him look hump-backed.

"What is your wish?" the King asked.

"I come to pray you that I may be made knight," said the young man, looking about him with keen interest.

"I see no reason why not," answered the King lightly. "What is your name?"

"Breunor le Noire, fair sire."

There was a mocking laugh behind them, and there was Sir Kay, the seneschal, grinning and pointing. Ever Sir Kay mocked at young men and boastful knights, for he said that if a man might not endure being laughed at he would never endure the more noble things as battle and death. Howbeit, Sir Kay was often unkind.

"Let us call him La Cote Male Taile," he cried, "the man with the ill-cut coat."

"Be quiet, Sir Kay," King Arthur chided him, and then turned to the young man, who had reddened but stood his ground. "Tell me why your coat hangs so, for sure am I that some adventure attaches to you."

"Sire," said Breunor, "my father, a right noble knight, had been hunting in the forest and was weary and laid him down to sleep. As he slept, his enemy came and foully murdered him. His coat was so cut and torn that it hangs like this, but I will wear it as it is till I am avenged. You, sire, they call the noblest knight in the world, so fain would I be made a knight by you."

"Yes, sire, make him a knight," said Sir Lamorak and Sir Gaheris, who were standing by. "He will be a good man and a mighty fighter."

King Arthur smiled. "You have support," he said. "But I too am on your side and tomorrow will I do it!"

But on the morrow a man came crying that he had put up a great hart in the woodlands and so the King and many knights rode eagerly to the chase. It was very quiet when they were all gone, so Breunor went into the garden, where Queen Guinevere was cutting a few late flowers. Those knights who had not gone

with King Arthur were talking or practising swordplay. At the far
end of the gardens were some cages in a stone tower, where were
kept strange beasts from pagan lands that had been sent as gifts to
the King. Among them was a lion, and it was roaring dolorously
and pacing in its place, as if wearying to escape.

Breunor walked along the pleasant paths and marvelled at the
flowers, for never had he seen so fair a display. He thought that
he could say with true worship that the fairest flower was Queen
Guinevere as she walked there with the golden sunshine on her
hair.

Right so came a mighty roaring, and the lion, which the gad-
flies had maddened, broke its rusty chain and smashed its cage
and came bounding out into freedom, its eyes like red coals, its
buff flanks heaving with excitement, its tufted tail switching to
and fro. A moment it stood so and then it leaped forward in great
bounds, its red jaws agape, and roaring as it came so that it was
a fearsome sight.

Queen Guinevere was a brave lady, but bravery in this case
would not have availed her. If she had stood her ground she
would have been struck down. There was a little postern near
at hand. Dropping her basket of flowers, the Queen made for its
cool shade and safety, with the lion bounding after her.

Of all the knights who had been there, barely a dozen remained;
the others had run out of the garden. The few left were too far
off and too palsied with the strangeness of the adventure to do
aught.

As the Queen reached shelter, only Breunor stood in the lion's
path.

"Sir Lion," cried Breunor, "I see now very plainly that there
are still many coward knights in this fair land. Now defend thee,
Sir Lion, for I will have ado with thee!"

Queen Guinevere, peeping from the safety of her doorway,
marvelled greatly at the young man's cool nerve, for he wore no
armour, but was still in his cloth-of-gold coat, which hung ill
upon his broad shoulders. Drawing his sword, he wrapped his
cloak about his left arm and so waited for the lion to come on.

With open jaws it leaped upon him, and he felt its warm
breath on his face; but he twisted aside and struck it with his

sword, slightly wounding it. Now was his danger increased more than ten times, for the beast was maddened.

"It is now or never," thought Breunor, and he heaved up his sword and smote the lion upon its head, even as its claws tore through his coat.

"That will sit upon my back more awry than before," murmured Breunor ruefully. "No matter; the beast is dead!"

Then men ran and told the Queen that La Cote Male Taile had rescued her, for she had not been able to stand and watch longer, but had run to her chamber. She came now, tearful and trembling, yet joyful at his bravery and much she grieved to see the red stains spreading steadily upon his coat.

With a winding of horns and a clattering of hooves, King Arthur and his knights rode into the courtyard.

"Oh, my fair lord," Queen Guinevere cried to him. "This boy who came here yesterday asking for knighthood today has done such a knightly deed as none other of these your men dared attempt." She related it all, and the knights who had run away looked abashed and ashamed.

King Arthur was overjoyed at this tale of prowess, and without a moment's delay he bade the young man kneel. Laying his sword lightly on his shoulder, he cried out: "Rise, Sir Breunor!"

Sir Breunor rose, and after he had thanked the King he turned to all the men assembled there. "I will not be called Sir Breunor," he said, smiling. "The name Sir Kay has given me likes me well, for it will be a remembrance to me of my request of revenge. Therefore, Sir La Cote Male Taile will I be, and all worshipful men shall call me so. Soon shall you hear of brave adventures, for if I can slay a lion then haply can I slay wicked creatures who walk on two legs."

"That shall we see!" said King Arthur.

CHAPTER 20

THE ADVENTURE OF
SIR LA COTE MALE TAILE

IT WAS on that very day that a lady came to the court seeking a knight.

"For what adventure do you seek him?" asked the King. "And why do you carry the shield? It has a strange device!"

All the knights stared at the shield in amazement, for it was ebon black in colour and in the middle was one white hand holding a sword.

"Who dares carry this shield will prove himself a mighty fighter," declared the lady. "I have borne it around until I am weary of it, but I have found no knight for it; he who carries it shall not lack adventure. It belonged to a good knight who was slain; ere he died, he told me that only at King Arthur's court should I find a man worthy of it."

"Ah, ha, my good knights!" cried King Arthur. "Here is a noble chance for one of you. Who will take the shield?" He gazed round him expectantly, but disappointment grew upon his face, for no man stepped forward. There was something terrifying in that sombre device, but had Sir Launcelot or Sir Tristram been there the shield would soon have had an owner.

Sir Kay picked it up, but the lady shook her head. "What is your name, fair sir?"

"Sir Kay, the seneschal! I should have thought you might have known it," he growled.

"That is a little matter, Sir Kay. What matters is that this adventure is not for you. A better man than you is needed."

"Lady," said Sir Kay haughtily. "I was but looking at the shield's device. I have no intention of going with you to seek adventure!" And he put the shield away from him in great annoyance.

Then the lady walked slowly down the line of knights and looked in their faces, as if to read their minds. Then she saw

Sir La Cote Male Taile and in her heart she loved him in that instant. Sorely was she afraid that he would want the adventure, for she did not wish to see him endangered, so much her heart warmed to him.

But he stepped forward. "Give me the shield!" he cried.

"No, no," she whispered. Aloud, she tried to dissuade him. "Your coat is ill-fitting, for I see that it has been badly cut; but if you take this shield, your skin will fare far worse than the cloth-of-gold!"

King Arthur came forward. "You are scarce full-grown," he said seriously. "A more hardy knight must speak up!" And he glanced round at his knights, none of whom, however, responded.

"I will take it," said Sir La Cote Male Taile, and he strode out and mounted and rode after the lady, bearing the shield right bravely on his shoulder.

"Do not follow me," she rebuked him, for she hoped that if she spoke harshly to him he might take offence and relinquish the adventure; for she was troubled for him.

Meanwhile Sir Kay called to him Sir Dagonet, the court jester. "Do something for me," he said. "That young hothead imagines that he is a great man because he slew a mangy old lion. Let us cool his ardour a little. Ride after him and joust with him and unhorse him; so will he look foolish!"

"I will well," said Sir Dagonet, who was always eager for a jest.

In a whirl of dust he galloped away through the red and gold of the autumn woods, and when he came up to the two he set up a great shouting.

"Turn and joust with me, Knight of the Shield Adventurous," he cried, and Sir La Cote Male Taile turned him and laid his spear in rest.

The two came together, and off his horse flew Sir Dagonet, to land with a crash in the bracken. He arose laughing, and took his horse and rode away.

"I suppose you think that that was worshipful and clever?" chided the lady, for to tell truth she had been terrified for her champion and yet, womanlike, would not show it. "That was the court jester, oh, mighty knight!"

"So I perceive," said La Cote Male Taile ruefully. "But this man looks more worthy of my lance."

She glanced up sharply and her heart failed. "No, no, not that knight. It is Sir Bleoberis himself," she gasped. "He is of Launcelot's kin and a great fighter!"

But Sir La Cote Male Taile prepared to joust with Sir Bleoberis, and the two came together. This time it was La Cote Male Taile who flew into the bracken, but he leaped up lightly to do further battle with his sword, for he was hurt and angry to have been unhorsed in front of the lady whom already he loved passing well.

"No, I will not fight you further," said Sir Bleoberis proudly and rode away.

Crestfallen, La Cote Male Taile caught his horse and mounted, and so relieved was his fair lady that she was inclined to jeer.

"Pray cease your jeers," he declared sadly. "I feel badly enough without your unkind words adding to it. I am not to blame because my horse went down before Sir Bleoberis's lance and threw me, and it is no shame to be unhorsed by such a knight. If it were, then there are many great men in like case with me!"

The next encounter he had was with the formidable Saracen, Sir Palamides, and again he went down into the dust. But Sir Palamides rode on and would not fight on foot. So Sir La Cote Male Taile was more depressed than ever and began to wonder if he were worthy to carry the Shield Adventurous, especially as his loved lady continued to rebuke him, for he did not know that in her heart she was afraid for him.

Sir Mordred, who was passing that way, joined them and so they rode through the lovely sunny woods, where at night there was a touch of early frost. After a while they saw before them a mighty castle called the Castle Orgulous, which spread its strong stone walls all across the valley meadows. Here there was a custom that travellers passing that way must joust with the men of the castle before they were allowed to travel on.

"Here come two strong fellows," said Sir Mordred. "You take the one and I will essay the other. The lady that rides with us shall await us in this little wood."

"That is well thought on," said Sir La Cote Male Taile.

Sir Mordred got the worst of his encounter, for the castle knight unhorsed him. The other two met so hardily that both went down, but they were soon up and remounted. La Cote Male Taile now turned his attention to Sir Mordred's opponent and he put him out of action with a spear thrust that would keep him in his bed for many days. Then he swung round his charger in time to see the other man fleeing towards the castle, so he followed him inside, and as they fought he by mischance killed him. It struck him then that it was a bad place in which to be surprised, for all around him rose the straight stone walls about the courtyard, and he could see no way out except by a gate and the narrow, echoing archway through which he had ridden in. His heart beat quicker as he saw that the arch was now black with advancing men; twenty knights on foot were marching on him; on his right were forty men, and on his left forty.

"Truly the Shield Adventurous is only for hardy knights," he muttered. Yet he told himself that he would rather die here in this grim courtyard in worshipful adventure than continue riding with the lady he loved so hopelessly, for she had no kind word for him.

Quickly he dismounted, for he did not wish his noble horse killed. He headed it towards the little gate and gave it a mighty slap so that it flourished its heels and galloped to safety. He put his back against the castle wall, gripped his sword, and began to fight as never he had dreamed he should be called upon to fight.

But fair eyes were on him, for at his back was a window, and there a lady sat and mused upon the battle. Presently she crept out of her chamber and round by a secret way outside the castle, and she caught his horse and lightly tied him by the postern gate which Sir La Cote Male Taile had seen. Then back she flew to watch again and greatly did she marvel that one man could do so much.

Her pity was great and at last she called out softly from the window so that only he, with his back against her wall, could hear.

"You are a noble knight," she whispered, "but you must die if you stay here! If you can work your way, even as you slash and stab, towards that postern, I have tied your horse there! But do not let your heart quail, for it will need the stoutest spirit in the world to win such worship as will come to him who can reach that gate with these wolves at his throat."

"Gramercy, fair helper," said Sir La Cote Male Taile, and with renewed courage he gripped his sword firmly and began to do as she advised, moving ever along the wall as he fought.

Inch by inch, he thrust his way. Not a stone of that old wall but saw such deeds as minstrels sing of. When he reached the postern he was red and grey with blood and dust, his armour was cracked, and his arm was so hot and weary he was near to fainting; but his heart was still undaunted. Four men were in front of him, having seen his ruse and rushed to cut him off. With two strokes he killed two of them and the others fell back aghast at such ferocity. Through the postern he sprang, leaped to his horse and so rode clean away.

In the meantime, Sir Mordred had gone back to the lady and found her trembling and unhappy.

"My foolish knight!" she said dolefully. "He must either be dead by now or in those castle dungeons."

"He comes now!" said Sir Mordred, when they had waited some time, and there indeed was La Cote Male Taile riding from the Castle Orgulous as if he had merely been upon a visit there.

"How did you escape?" cried she, and when he had told her, modestly enough, she could not credit it. Afterwards, men came and told her it was even so, for, said they, he was a devil and no man who could fight like that. Twelve knights were dead in there and many sorely wounded. Then was she very proud of him and sorry that she had seemed to taunt him, especially as Sir Mordred now scolded her for her sharpness.

"I will tell you all the truth of it," he said. "Those knights that overthrew him, Sir Bleoberis and Sir Palamides, are wily warriors. 'Tis easy to tell a young knight who has ridden little, because he sits not too firmly in the saddle. Such knights are easily unhorsed—but they are mostly wickedly dangerous on foot; and so a clever old knight will not essay a young one on foot, for many a proud and hardy knight has met his match with the sword when encountering a new, green knight who has yet to grow hairs upon his chin. That·was why those knights rode on—not because they despised Sir La Cote Male Taile, as you thought, but because they feared him! Now smile upon him, for he is a hero and you should encourage such a man to fight for his lady!"

"I will well," she replied, and she smiled on Sir La Cote Male Taile—to his great joy.

CHAPTER 21

THE CAPTURE AND RESCUE OF SIR LA COTE MALE TAILE

SIR LAUNCELOT got back to the court from one of his adventures and was distressed to hear that La Cote Male Taile had taken on the adventure of the black shield.

"I will ride after him," he said. "I think it was shameful of you older knights that not one stepped out and took the shield, but left a boy to shoulder it."

So he galloped after La Cote Male Taile and the lady. When Sir Mordred saw more company coming, he rode away. Sir Launcelot saluted the other two, but the lady did not know who it was. She was again trying to turn her champion from going any farther, using all her wiles on him and rebuking him when he would not listen. Poor Sir La Cote Male Taile was answering in a knightly, gentle way, for he loved her so and did not wish to offend her; but Sir Launcelot had no such scruples, and he answered her back, reproof for reproof, at which she left off teasing La Cote Male Taile, turning on the other and speaking him hardly, which she would not have done if she had known who he was. Troubled for her own knight-errant, she recked little what she said.

Sir Launcelot appeared to find it all right mirthful, and so they rode a long way, arguing, until he had to leave them for a while, but promising that he would join them again. The lady and her knight rode on and reached the Castle of Pendragon.

"There will surely be adventure here," said Sir La Cote Male

Taile, "for whenever the black shield is seen there is always someone will attempt some small encounter for his worship."

"There are six knights before the big gate," said the lady uneasily. "One of them is proffering himself to joust. Need you meet him? Can we not go some other way?"

"Nay, nay," he answered. "We must take what chance we meet!"

So he galloped forward, head low, spear aimed, and plumes fluttering. One of the six rode out to joust with him and Sir La Cote Male Taile sent him flying over his horse's tail. Then he turned him to see if perchance any other of the knights would like to adventure his person. His heart gave a queer little thrill of fear, for all five were setting on him at once, and where a man could take on great numbers of men on foot as he had done he was nearly helpless with those five murderous spears all pointing straight at his heart as the knights charged down in dust and thunder upon him. But he would rather have been hewn in pieces than turn tail, so he urged his horse to a gallop, picked out the nearest knight to aim at, and set his teeth.

There was a crash and shock, a squealing of horses and a splintering of lances, and in the tumble and confusion La Cote Male Taile was down, stunned and breathless. The five men leaped from their horses and all fell upon him to take him prisoner. They led him, bruised and shaken, into the gloomy courts of Pendragon Castle and down into a straw carpeted dungeon where rats squeaked and rustled incessantly. And there he sat and took his singing head in his hands and wondered ruefully what was to become of him and what the lady was doing without him, and he sighed right dolefully.

Meanwhile Sir Launcelot came pricking along to overtake them again, and he fell in with a knight whom he knew and they had a little friendly spear-running and then chatted as they sat and cooled off.

"Go not past Pendragon Castle," advised Sir Nerovens, "for there is a very strong knight there, its owner, and he has many men in the castle, all of them dangerous, hardy fighters who will take on anyone. I hear that they caught a knight yesterday and took him prisoner. He was riding with a lady in search of adventure!"

"Surely that must be Sir La Cote Male Taile, who is a friend of mine," said Sir Launcelot. "I will ride to the rescue at once, so I pray you will excuse me. Plenty of time has been lost already if it was yesterday that he was taken."

He set out with all speed, riding straight for Pendragon Castle, for he was 'afraid of nothing. As he neared the place, the six knights came out as before, and as before they all prepared to set on him at once in most unknightly fashion. But they had other metal against them this time; the greatest fighter in the world was charging down upon them.

Launcelot's spear caught the foremost man with so murderous and well-aimed a blow that his back was broken. Launcelot himself never seemed to feel that three of the spears had splintered on his own shield, for he was rock-like in the saddle. The other two knights missed their aim. He was through the pack of them now, but round he came with a graceful caracole and down upon them he charged again like an avenger. His spear went right through one of the men, to stand out behind his back, but the spear broke. Then the four men that were left drew their swords and with cries of rage and menace they sought to close about him. Just four strokes it took Sir Launcelot to unhorse four knights and then he rode full tilt, with a mighty clatter of hooves, right into the castle court. There emerged the lord of the castle, Sir Brian of the Isles, a fine fighter, but an enemy of King Arthur's.

"Ha, sir knight, defend yourself," he said, "as you have thus ventured under my portcullis."

And they fought very hardily, for well-matched were they. But as well might a candle seek to outshine the sun as for Sir Brian to hope to win an encounter with the matchless Sir Launcelot. He was beaten to his knees at last, and his opponent tore off his helm to kill him, but he yielded to him and asked for grace and mercy.

"Will you deliver all your prisoners free from your dungeons? Open up, sir knight, open up!"

Door after door was unlocked and out filed the prisoners, some of them famous men who had lain there for many weeks, and many ladies of high worship.

Sir Launcelot rode on without seeing Sir La Cote Male Taile, but he was among the men who came out blinking into the autumn sunlight like so many owls. They found their horses and arms, and Sir La Cote Male Taile found his lady waiting for him, and passing glad was she to see him, and he her. And they were then told who it was who had freed them all and that it was also the man who had ridden with them a few days before.

"Ah, woe is me!" cried the lady. "How I rebuked him! Had I known who it was I had held my foolish tongue and listened instead with bated breath to his stories of great adventures. Come quickly; let us overtake him that I may say how sorry I am!"

It was not long before they came up with their rescuer, and she did even as she had said. "Oh, and let us ride with you, for never did I think to have this honour," she finished.

"On one condition," said Sir Launcelot, smiling upon her when he remembered some of the things she had said, "that you will not missay this good knight more!"

Then did she tell him tearfully how dearly she loved her champion and how she trembled for him and tried to put him off from jousting lest he come to harm.

"It was a kindly thought of yours," he said, "but, in truth, unwise, for you made him only the more eager. I have thought of you as the lady with the unkind tongue, but now you shall be the lady with the loving heart."

That day they came to a fortress. Then said Sir La Cote Male Taile: "There will be adventures here, I wot; prithee, let me essay first. This is surely an adventure of my shield."

"I like you not to go in first," said Sir Launcelot dubiously, but the other begged so hard that he agreed.

So Sir La Cote Male Taile rode forward against two men who barred the way. Long time they fought, he alone against the two of them and ever they tried to outflank him, but with great cunning he kept them before him and though sorely wounded at length forced them to yield.

Then came another knight, Sir Plenorius, against him. And as he was not fresh, Sir La Cote Male Taile was gradually weakened and overcome so that he sank to the earth all faint with loss of blood, for he had been battling for hours. Sir

Launcelot and the lady sat and watched and marvelled at his great prowess.

Sir Plenorius took pity on Sir La Cote Male Taile and spoke him very knightly. "Fair sir," he said, "if you had been fresh when I encountered with you, you would have beaten me long ago. Come, gentle knight, lean on my arm and I will take you into my castle and you shall have wine and meat and ointment for your wounds!"

"I thank you kindly," said the other, "but if you have stomach for even more fighting then go back to where I met the two knights and there you will find one who is indeed worthy of your lance."

So Sir Plenorius helped him into his castle and sent men quickly to see to him. Right so he said: "Now will I go encounter with this other knight who is of your fellowship and if he is as doughty as you were I shall have a famous fight with him."

Just as he was about to go out he heard a voice like a trumpet calling.

"Sir Plenorius, where are you? Set free that prisoner that you have taken within, or come out here that I may have ado with you!"

Sir Plenorius rushed out eagerly to do battle, but now he had met his match and he was driven relentlessly back till he was fighting just outside his own tower gate.

"Sir Plenorius," said Sir Launcelot, as they fought, "you are a good knight. Yield you to me!"

But the other would not, and only fought harder than ever, and he struck Sir Launcelot such a blow on the helm that it seemed as if fire sprang out of his eyes. But he had to yield at the last.

"I will ask King Arthur to give you a seat at the Round Table," said Sir Launcelot, as he sheathed his sword, and no higher praise of his might could Sir Plenorius have had, and he was right joyful because of it.

Then they all went into his castle and there they were until such time as Sir La Cote Male Taile was well again. And they had a merry time and games and pleasant rest.

At the next feast of Pentecost both Sir Plenorius and Sir La Cote Male Taile were made Knights of the Round Table and all said that the young man was a worthy bearer of the black shield. He married the lady and they were very happy together, she even encouraging and helping him in his knightly deeds. In years to come, so the tale runs, he revenged his noble father, for whom he had worn the coat which was so badly slashed.

This is the end of the story of Sir La Cote Male Taile, called by rights Sir Breunor Le Noire!

CHAPTER 22

THE COMING OF SIR PERCIVALE

SIR TOR, the son of King Pellinore, had a younger brother called Percivale, and when he was old enough to be made knight he had no wish for anything but that it should be King Arthur who should dub him, for he longed to go to Camelot and serve him.

Sir Tristram had departed and gone back to Ireland with King Mark, and all the knights felt his loss, for they had all loved him and his going left a gap in their ranks. The Queen missed him too, and as she sat at her embroidery she thought sadly of him, for she pitied him for his wretchedness in that he loved Isoud the Beautiful.

In her secret heart, Queen Guinevere knew that her own case was the same. For many long years now she had loved Sir Launcelot, and she knew that it was wrong of her not to fight this love, for she owed her loyalty to her husband. Launcelot loved her in return, but in giving way to this love for King Arthur's wife he laid the first tarnish upon the shining glory of his knighthood.

Seated at the Queen's feet, sorting her silks and wools, was a sweet-faced maiden, born of a noble house and come to be an attendant on the Queen at Camelot. She was dumb, and had been so from birth, but Guinevere loved her dearly and often talked to her at length, easing her own pain in sharing what was in her mind.

"They say that a new knight has come to court and been received by King Arthur," the Queen told her maiden. "His name is Sir Percivale. I wonder what great deeds he will do?"

At the name, the little maiden looked up, and her eyes were shining.

"What do you know of him?" smiled the Queen.

The child shook her head, meaning that she knew nothing; but everyone at court believed that she had gifts of intuition that revealed to her much of what was to be.

Later, the Queen went to King Arthur where he sat among his knights and asked about Percivale.

"Sir Percivale?" the King answered. "I made him knight this day, but methinks it will be long before he wins much honour, for he is a dreamer."

"I never saw a man less fitted for knighthood," agreed a knight. "But 'tis not safe to judge by outward show. Let us remember Beaumains and Sir La Cote Male Taile."

"When shall I see him?" said the Queen, with interest.

"Tonight at dinner come into the hall, for he will be there," said King Arthur.

So Queen Guinevere was down in the great oak hall betimes as the knights were filing in and finding their places about the Round Table. At the lower end of the hall were other tables for those knights who were not of the Table Round. They were ranked as they were worthy, the worshipful men at the higher end, and knights of less honour at the lower.

King Arthur came in talking to Sir Launcelot and Sir Aglavale. Following quietly was a gentle-faced boy who certainly looked as if he were more used to reading monkish manuscripts than practising with lances or learning to master horses.

"Where shall Sir Percivale sit?" asked a steward of the King. "You have not yet assigned him a place, sire!"

Arthur considered, and then pointed down to the lower table against the wall. "Set him there," he said. "He is like the others and must work his own way by his own prowess, and as yet he is unproven and untried. Though he is King Pellinore's son, I cannot for that show him greater indulgence than other men have had."

"What a fair face!" Queen Guinevere whispered.

"A face will not win him worship," replied King Arthur.

Sir Percivale went quietly to his place and sat down. The King called for the meat to be served; but before the serving lads could advance with the trenchers of bread and the roast joints and capons, the door at the end of the hall swung open and the Queen's little dumb maiden entered. Very childish she looked, with her long plaits of hair hanging down and her little face pale.

"Child, what do you here?" Queen Guinevere asked gently.

The maiden smiled at her and then stood looking along the lines of knights, calm and unhurried as if someone had given her some mission to perform, and she wanted to fulfil it perfectly. Then she saw what she sought and walked down to the lower table. All stared at her and marvelled at her gentleness and calm.

Straight up to Sir Percivale she went and held out one thin little hand. Then in a clear treble, sweet as birdsong at even, she spoke aloud—the maiden who had been dumb from birth. Even the hardiest there were startled. Queen Guinevere's face went white, for there was something not worldly about the happening. None guessed that a great chapter in the Round Table story was beginning, and that the Quest of the Holy Grail would soon begin, though none knew about it as yet.

"Rise, Sir Percivale," she said slowly. "Rise and follow where I shall lead you. You are God's knight and His work is ready to be done. Come, for this is not your place!"

He rose to follow her, though he seemed perplexed. She led him right up to the Round Table near to the Siege Perilous, which had stood empty all these long years.

"Here, next to the Siege Perilous," she told him, "is an empty place. It is yours, and you shall sit beside the greatest knight of all time. He is not yet come, but he will come! He will fill this place where only the worthiest may be."

Wonderingly, Sir Percivale looked across at King Arthur.

Though the maiden had spoken with authority, he yet felt unworthy to seat himself there among the greatest company of knights in the world. But the King nodded and signalled to him to do as the maiden said, and so Sir Percivale was made one of the Round Table fellowship on his second day at King Arthur's court and before he had done a single deed to prove himself.

CHAPTER 23

THE VISIONS OF SIR BORS

THERE was a knight at the court in those days called Sir Bors de Ganis, nephew of Sir Launcelot, and though he knew it not he was one of the three men who by their nobility of knighthood and godly living were deemed worthy to achieve the Quest of the Holy Grail. Many set out upon the quest, as shall soon be told, but many returned, many grew weary and gave up the search, and many died.

Sir Bors had been bidden to pay a visit to an old friend, King Pelles, of Corbin Castle. As yet, he thought little of the future and what might befall him. He was happy enough to take adventures as they came to him, but he was just and gentle, and never fought merely to advance his own honour and glory, but only when there was a good deed to do, someone to rescue from peril, or some old and wicked custom to stamp out.

He felt little fear as he neared King Pelles's castle, though it was a place with a queer reputation. Strange adventures had come to visiting knights who slept within its frowning walls. Men said that only those whose lives were pure departed thence with honour.

Sir Gawaine had just visited, and he had left in a great hurry, for though a brave knight and a good companion he was selfish and much given to earthly vanities.

King Pelles knew Sir Bors and welcomed him. Dining together, they fell to talking of the old castle.

"They call this the Castle Adventurous," Sir Bors mused.
"Why is that, fair sir?"

King Pelles smiled as he told him, and added: "Son, take
my advice and lie this night in the village beyond the castle
dykes. Only the very hardiest can endure some of the strange
and ghostly things that happen here."

"I think I would like to stay here, if it please you," said Sir
Bors quietly. "I believe that there is here some lesson for me
to learn and that I was led here of a purpose!"

Later, a priest took him into the castle chapel. Here many
a knight had watched his armour in lonely vigil through the
night. It was cold as death in there, for the great stone walls
were twelve feet thick, and though the altar blazed with candles
no heat seemed to come from them.

Sir Bors was then taken by the priest to a chamber where he
should sleep. It was nearly as cold in there as in the chapel,
and he began to feel afraid. It was a great eight-sided room
and in each wall was a door. Sir Bors wondered what lay behind
those doors. But he was tired and the big bed looked inviting.
He did not unarm himself, but lay for a long time staring into
the darkness. If he could not endure the ghosts and phantasies
of a vision, he reflected, how could he endure the test of fleshly
adventure?

Then suddenly the room was illumined, so that he could see
about him. He sat up. The light came from the head of a great
spear, which seemed to be burning. It was coming straight towards him, and he felt a stab of agony in his shoulder, as if the
spear's flaming head had pierced him.

So fearful was the pain that he sank down upon the bed
again. Then he thought that a knight came in through one of
the doors and challenged him and that they fought long, and
ever he tried to come between the knight and the door through
which he had come. At length the knight departed.

Then there was a terrible sound, louder than summer thunder,
and the wail and rattle as of deadly hail. All the doors flew
open as if a storm wind were blowing upon them, and the air
was filled with flight after flight of arrows, which fell thickly
upon him and seemed to wound him sore.

In his heart he prayed for strength to act the man and not show himself a coward in face of this curious visitation. Then out of the gloom, glowing with its own light, came a vision of a mighty lion, which seemed to float roaring through the air.

Sir Bors put his shield before him and gripped his sword.

"Now God defend me!" he whispered devoutly, but with one blow of his paw the lion whipped his shield aside, and put its great foaming jaws at his throat.

Sir Bors heaved up his sword and struck out bravely, and, lo, he killed the beast with one blow, and suddenly it faded and was gone.

Then a great storm wind began to blow and howl and scream about the castle, so that a man could scarce have heard his own voice above it. Sir Bors's heart turned to ice, for a dragon of frightening aspect suddenly appeared. Then came a snarling leopard, which attacked the dragon. The two fought long and fiercely.

Many and strange were the visions that followed, but Sir Bors endured them all, and ever the storm screamed about the castle walls. Then finally came a silver-haired man, who played upon a harp, and he sang to the watching knight.

Then he said: "Leave this place now, Sir Bors, for day is almost come and there will be no more adventures for you. You have done right well and worshipfully and have fought a greater terror than any vision which has here assailed you—and that is human fear. The future holds greater adventures for you. Return to Sir Launcelot and tell him all that you have seen and done. Alas and alas that he cannot achieve the holy deeds that you, and such as you, can do!"

Then it seemed to Sir Bors that he asked the old man a question, for it grieved him to hear this of Sir Launcelot.

"You ask why he shall not also have honour in the quest?" was the grave reply. "Because of forbidden love. Alas, he could have passed all earthly men in knightly greatness but for this one grievous sin."

Then suddenly the storm wind ceased to howl and there fell a silence so profound that it was as if the world held its breath. Into the darkness came a white dove, burning as if with a white

E

fire. In its bill was a golden censer and from this came sweetest odours, which trailed about it like a cloud of white smoke. Then came a clearness, as if some celestial light were burning.

Sir Bors kneeled him down and bowed his head and closed his eyes reverently, for it was said that the dove and the censer were seen before the vision of the Holy Grail. His limbs trembled, but his heart was full of thankful joy for the honour which was done to him.

When he looked up again, he saw an altar and figures kneeling, and a bishop bending before the altar; the light grew ever more and more brilliant till no human eyes could bear its radiance. And he saw a white-robed figure bearing the Holy Grail. So he fell forward fainting and could no more see, for he was blinded.

A long time after, when his swoon had passed and his sight returned to him, he found himself back upon his bed. The dawn was breaking, birds were singing outside, and all the beauty of a summer morning greeted him.

He rose and met King Pelles, his friend, and told him all that he had seen, and both made great joy of each other. Then Sir Bors returned to Camelot and told Sir Launcelot, as he had been bidden. Sir Launcelot was troubled in his heart at what Sir Bors said, for he loved Queen Guinevere, and could not give her up. He and she met secretly, and King Arthur, trusting them, suspected nothing.

CHAPTER 24

THE QUEST OF THE HOLY GRAIL

Now began the Quest of the Holy Grail. For long it had been thought that somewhere upon earth existed the vessel which Jesus had used at the Last Supper, when the wine in it was blest and given to the disciples to drink. It was called the Holy Grail. Many had sought for the Holy Grail in years gone by, but without success.

There came to King Arthur's court one day a lady, who asked for Sir Launcelot.

"He is there," said the King, smiling as he pointed to him.

Sir Launcelot sat apart, his chin upon his cupped hands, his countenance grave, as if his thoughts were heavy.

"What do you want with me?" he asked her, raising his dark eyes to search her face.

"Follow me," she said, "for I will bring you to a place where there is work for you to do!"

"Lead on," said Sir Launcelot. "As soon as my horse is saddled, I will attend you!"

As they were leaving, the Queen swept down the stone stairway, and at sight of Sir Launcelot's departing, as she thought, upon some adventure, she gave a cry of distress.

"Are you leaving us?" she said, and she ran to him and clasped his arm.

The lady looked on her with pity and comforted her. "To-morrow he will be back," she said.

"If it were not so, I should not let him go," murmured Queen Guinevere.

Through a thick forest rode Launcelot and the lady, and it was passing fair, for the early flowers were budding bravely and the red squirrels chattered and played in the pines. Soon they came in sight of a white building with a tower, in which hung a bell, for it was a nunnery.

"There is a youth here that the nuns have brought up and 'trained in all manner of goodness. He is to be made a knight this day and by your hands, for so it has been arranged!" said the lady. "Two brother knights of yours are staying here, Sir Bors and Sir Lionel, and they will make great joy that you are come!"

It was even so, for Sir Launcelot found them resting in an upstairs room, and he waked them. They went down together and stood talking in the raftered hall. Then in came twelve nuns, and they were weeping, for the whitest hope of all their little flock was to leave them.

Walking in the midst of them came Galahad, and his countenance was so unearthly fair that Sir Launcelot was startled and greatly troubled.

"Oh, fair sir, make this gentle youth a knight," said the nuns. "We have taught him all we can, and now he must out and away into the great world to do those deeds that God has prepared for him!"

"Does *he* wish it?" asked Launcelot, gazing in growing wonder at the pure, serene face.

"Yes," said Galahad. "It is my wish!"

So Launcelot made him a knight, and then he looked at him almost sadly, as if seeing in him something that he himself would never now attain.

"God make you a good man," he muttered. "Strength and beauty and purity you have more than any man I ever saw. I had them all once, even as you. Goodness only is needed to make you great. Do you ride with me now to King Arthur's court?"

"Not yet," said Galahad. "The time is not quite come!"

It so happened that at Pentecost the King was about to sit down to meat when Sir Kay plucked his sleeve. "What, brother, will you break an old custom of yours? Shall we not wait for some adventure?"

"Sooth you say," said King Arthur. "Let us wait and see what comes. Methinks this squire who comes running has already somewhat of import to tell us!"

"Sire," gasped the young man in excitement, for he was delighted to be the one to find the King's Pentecost wonder, "sire, in the river is a great stone, a stone floating as if it were simple wood. In it is a sword."

"Let us haste and see it," said the King.

Sure enough, there lay upon the river's dimpled surface a block of red marble. The sword impaled in it had a hilt encrusted with precious stones. On it in letters of gold were words declaring that only the finest knight in all the world should take the sword and wear it.

"Then must it be yours," cried King Arthur, in generous joy, turning to Sir Launcelot.

But the great knight stood looking at it, and shook his head. None guessed what sober thoughts occupied his mind.

"It is not mine," he said sadly. "Whoso touches that sword

unworthily and who has no right to it will be wounded grievously by it, for so it says in the ancient books."

King Arthur looked greatly disappointed, and he gazed at Launcelot in surprise. Never had he heard his favourite knight talk so. He sighed, then turned to his nephew, Sir Gawaine.

"Try it, Sir Gawaine, for love of me," he urged.

Sir Gawaine shook his head. "That may not be," he muttered.

"It is a command!" cried the King, and the royal temper in him began to flash in his eyes.

"Sire, if it is a command," returned Sir Gawaine, "it is but for me to obey."

He laid his hand to the sword, but he could not stir it from where it was fixed in the marble.

"Sir Gawaine," said Launcelot seriously, "now you have tried and failed. You will be so hurt because of this that you will wish you had died rather than touch it."

"It was a command," said Gawaine quietly.

King Arthur was much upset to hear these words, but still he could not let the matter alone. "Sir Percivale," he begged, "you are a good knight and fearless. Essay this thing for me."

"I will," answered Sir Percivale, smiling, "out of comradeship for Sir Gawaine. He and I will suffer together!" And so he tried, but he could not move the sword from the stone.

After that, no one else dared to come forward.

"Let us now dine," said Sir Kay, "for surely this is the strangest thing we have ever seen!"

Back to the castle they tramped and filed into the great dining-hall, where the boys and young knights had just finished setting all things ready on the Round Table. Five score and fifty places were set, but, as usual, only five score and forty-nine knights went to their places, for no one sat in the Siege Perilous. The serving knights carried round the food, and each man's trencher was filled.

Suddenly, all the doors into the hall and all the window-shutters closed of themselves. A strange half-light filled the place and all talk was hushed. Each man looked in his neighbour's face and read there the wonder that he himself felt. Then the valves of the main door opened again soundlessly and in came two men, one old but with a stately face as of a king and hair like December frost. By his side walked a young knight in red armour, but without sword or shield, though an empty scabbard dangled at his hip.

"Peace be with you," said the red knight.

The old man presented his charge to King Arthur.

"You are surely welcome," said the King, in wonder.

"Doff your armour," said the old man, and the red knight unarmed himself and laid his suit of plate, piece by piece, upon the flags. Underneath he wore a suit of red sendel, very fine.

The old man threw a furred mantle about his shoulders, then led him to the Round Table.

All present held their breath, for they realised suddenly that only the one place was vacant, that between Sir Launcelot and Sir Percivale, the Siege Perilous. Straight to it went the old man and lifted up the broidered cover which was always upon it. King Arthur's breath caught in his throat, for he was remembering Merlin's words, spoken all those years and years ago.

"This," said the old man, "this is the siege of Galahad, who has come to be among you."

Having said this he went quietly out of the hall and was seen no more.

Then those men, hardy, adventurous, some reckless, some fool-hardy, all sat and stared in silent awe at this calm-faced lad, this young knight who had been privileged to seat himself in the Siege Perilous. Those who had essayed this over the years had all come to grievous woe for their presumption. But Sir Galahad seemed to think it natural enough, and he ate the food that was set before him, and heeded not the glances that fell upon him.

When all were risen, King Arthur hurried round to him and looked at the Siege Perilous; and there in letters of gold had appeared the name GALAHAD.

"This is a great marvel!" cried the King. "You are he who was foretold. And it was said that you should begin the Quest of the Holy Grail, and achieve it. Come with me, I pray you, young sir, and essay the adventure of the stone down in the river hard by!"

All the court went with them, curiosity strong. Queen Guinevere and all her ladies, shimmering in silks and ermine-edged mantles of cloth-of-gold, wended their way in haste down the grassy, daisied ways from the castle.

"Here is the marvel," said the King and he pointed to the floating stone and the sword still stuck therein. "No man can move it!"

Sir Galahad looked at the King and there was an expression on his face so wonderful that all who saw it remembered it all his life.

"That is no marvel," said Galahad. "This adventure was not theirs, but mine." He drew the sword and sheathed it in his empty scabbard. "Methinks it is better there than in the stone," he said.

"You have no shield," said King Arthur. "Surely God will send you that also!"

At that moment the crowd parted and a lady rode forward on a white horse. She was weeping.

"Where is Sir Launcelot?" she cried, and her voice trembled by reason of her tears.

"I am here, fair lady," he answered, surprised.

"Ah, woe, that your estate is so changed from only this morning," she sobbed.

"I am the same," he said, his black brows drawn together in a frown.

"You have lost your place for ever and for ever," she went on, weeping. "Long years have you held it and now it is yours no more! You were the best knight in all the world until today, and now a greater one stands before you. Never call yourself so again!"

Sir Launcelot drew himself up proudly. "I never called myself so before," he answered. "I knew right well I was never the best!"

"Yes, you were, and as earthly men are reckoned, you still are! But the quest is upon you all and a sign is coming to you to encourage you all."

She departed as she had come and she left all the people silent and wondering.

"Much honour is being done to us," King Arthur said solemnly. "But in this I see the end of our glorious fellowship approaching, for I shall never again see you all again together at one time at my table. Into far lands are you going. Many will give up their lives. Sieges will be empty at the Round Table, and the gold letters of noble names will fade away and be no more."

Then did the King ordain that there should be a jousting held that afternoon. He had a secret reason for saying this, for he wished to see if Sir Galahad were worthy, as no man had seen him proved.

"You will joust also," he commanded Galahad. "Don your arms and then come to me and I will let you have a shield of mine, as you have none."

"I will have no shield, sire," said Sir Galahad, "but I will come and joust, as you require me!" And nothing the King could say would make the young man borrow a shield.

The Queen and all her ladies came to watch as the knights assembled in the lists, and Galahad was given a spear. He rode to the centre of the place and sat on his horse waiting quietly for them to come against him. The afternoon sun lay golden upon his red armour so that he seemed to burn with a strange fire.

No man could stand against him when the jousting began, save only two, Sir Launcelot and Sir Percivale.

"Call him to me," said the Queen when the test was over. "Fain would I see him near me."

"Come hither," Arthur commanded. "Unhelm you, sir knight."

Guinevere looked long and wonderingly into his face, but none knew what she saw there or what regret and remorse beset her for her own failings as she beheld his goodness and purity.

As they sat at supper that night, with all the five score and fifty sieges filled, a storm of thunder broke over Camelot so fierce that in the memory of man nothing like it had been heard. It was night, the sun long since having gone to rest, so that all were startled as a pure sunbeam fell into the vast hall and upon the bowed heads of the knights. Then, floating above them in the glorious light, came the vision of the Holy Grail. It was screened from their sight by a cloth of white samite, but from it darted rays of light that waxed and receded as lightning seems to do. Over their heads it passed slowly, and so it passed and was gone.

"Only one thing was not permitted us," said Sir Gawaine sorrowfully. "The Holy Grail was so covered that our eyes could not see it. Here and now, before you all, I vow that tomorrow I will set forth and seek for it wherever it may be, searching for it diligently. No matter if it be weeks or months or years, still will I seek. If it is denied me, then I will return to you knowing that it is not my quest."

With a rustle of coats of gold and velvet and the swish of silks, all the knights of the Round Table rose and joined their vows to his. Great joy uplifted all their hearts, but the King was very sorrowful for he saw the fellowship breaking up, never again to be complete.

Sir Launcelot tried to comfort him, for he said: "Remember that you always wanted us to earn true honour. How can we earn it better than dying in this quest?"

But King Arthur would not be comforted, nor the Queen, nor all the ladies of the court.

Few slept well that night. The knights furbished their arms and there was a great work in the castle. Torches were burned down and replenished with new ones, which in their turn burned down to the sockets as preparations went forward for the quest of the Holy Grail.

In the cool grey morning light the knights marched out of the castle and along the streets to the minster. They were fully armed except for helms and shields, and the people lined up to see them pass. Flaxen-haired, brown-haired, dark-haired, their armour shining, the knights marched.

After the service the great war-horses were led out, all caparisoned and armed, and the knights donned their helms. Mournfully the rooks called round the towers of Camelot as the cavalcade set out, while rich and poor wept to see it go by. The King could not speak for sorrow.

They rode, one hundred and fifty strong, until Camelot was far behind them. Only adventure lay before them. Then they parted, each knight set out along the way he thought the best. So upon that fair Whit Monday morning began the Quest of the Holy Grail.

CHAPTER 25

SIR GALAHAD

FOR FOUR days Sir Galahad rode fully armed upon the quest, but still without a shield. At first no adventure came to him, but he rode on, coming at last to an abbey in a lonely land where streams wended their way through meadows starred with wild forget-me-not.

"I will rest here for the night," Sir Galahad said, for he loved the peace of such places more than the torchlight and noise of castle courts.

He was received by the monks hospitably, for the quest was bringing many knights-errant to the abbey. The exciting news they brought broke the monotony of the good fathers' lives.

"There are already two of your fellows of the Round Table here," they told Sir Galahad, and in the refectory he soon met them: King Bagdemagus and Sir Uwaine.

"What adventures have you had?" he asked them eagerly.

"None as yet, but we hope for some tomorrow," the King answered. "Have you not heard? In this abbey a most worthy shield is hung, yet it belongs to nobody. Only the hardiest and bravest would dare to hang it about his neck, for if unworthily borne it would bring mischief to the wearer. I shall try it tomorrow. If I fail, you may essay it."

"I will well," answered Galahad, "for I have no shield of my own."

Next morning King Bagdemagus asked to be shown the shield, and he and Galahad were led to where it hung in the shadows, gleaming white, with a broad blood-red cross upon it.

"You know the penalty?" they were warned. "Take not this adventure too rashly on you, for only the most worthy knight can take it safely!"

King Bagdemagus hesitated and stroked his beard. "I know right well that there are many more worthy knights than I," he said soberly, but the fire of daring was burning in him and his eyes were alight with excitement. He walked forward boldly. "I will essay this thing!" he cried. With hands that trembled a little he lifted down the shield and carried it outside to where his horse stood waiting. Then he turned to Sir Galahad. "You shall stay here so that you may hear how it is with me."

"I will await you," was the quiet answer. "Take with you this honest boy as squire and he shall bring me news of you again."

So King Bagdemagus rode away, carrying the great shield proudly. The birds sang, and all seemed fair.

"See, over yonder comes a horseman," cried his squire, "a brave and noble-looking knight, galloping towards us as fast as his horse can travel. His spear is in rest. He seems to wish to have ado with you!"

"Adventure comes quickly this morning," said King Bagdemagus, and for a moment, perhaps, he wondered if he had been a little bold in carrying off the shield. Still, he had asked for adventure, so he must take it when it came. He laid his own spear in rest and spurred forward.

There was something ominous in the determined rush towards him of the knight, who was clad entirely in white armour. The King's spear splintered to pieces on his opponent's shield, but it had no more effect than if a fly had brushed past the other's face. He himself was not so lucky, for the white knight's spear smashed his shoulder armour and wounded him badly, so that he fell in a faint off his horse.

The white knight dismounted, stalked across to him, and took up the white shield.

"You did great folly in taking on this adventure," he said hardly. "This shield is for a nobler knight." He swung round and faced the King's squire. "Take this in charge and carry it back to Sir Galahad, who alone may wear it."

Then the white knight rode away, with never a glance at the poor headstrong king, who lay groaning on the ground.

"How is it with you, sir?" asked his squire, in great distress.

"Help me on my horse," said the King. "It may happen that I can ride far enough to get somewhere where my wound can be dressed and seen to, but it will be many a long day before I can proceed on my quest."

So the two returned, and the squire carried the red-crossed shield, sorely afraid of it.

Sir Galahad received it gladly. "Now am I fully armed," he said. "Now can I go forward!" Almost at once Sir Galahad found service to his hand and occupied himself with many deeds of knight-errantry. One morning he came out on a hillside and saw, in a valley before him, a strong castle with deep ditches all about it. It stood on the banks of the River Severn. An old man was hobbling up the road, and Sir Galahad drew rein.

"What place is that?" he asked, shading his eyes against the sun to gaze at the great pile, the lofty walls and keep of which rose sheer two hundred feet without an arrow-slit or window.

"Fair sir, that is called the Castle of Maidens," he was told. "It is a cursed castle and within it are many poor prisoners, who have long ago given up hope of rescue. It would need a king's army to take such a fortalice!"

Sir Galahad sat his horse and looked upon it where it gloomed black against the skyline.

"It would seem that there is work for me to do," he answered calmly.

The old fellow came to him and clutched his stirrup. "Turn away, sir knight," he counselled. "What can you do, one feeble lance against stone walls as thick as those?"

"Now wit ye well, I shall not turn away from those who need me," said the red-cross knight.

He looked to his arms carefully, then spurred his horse forward. Seven maidens were coming slowly up the hill, chattering and laughing and looking with interest at the stern-looking figure riding down to them, his horse's hooves clipping and clattering among the loose stones. They seemed a little dismayed too, for one of them called out to him.

"This is no road for you, sir knight, for that is an evil castle, where the men will slay you as a stranger, and you have the river to cross."

"Well, maidens," he smiled at them, "why should I not cross the river?"

They stood and watched him in wonder as he went on, the sunlight flashing from his white shield. Soon he met a squire, who cried haughtily: "I bear a defiance from the men of the castle. You shall ride no farther until I hear why you are upon this road."

"I am coming to free the castle," Galahad answered mildly, as if it was merely a matter of opening a door and letting the folk out.

"You have indeed enough work before you," returned the squire, astonished. "I thought not to hear of a single-knight-errant attempting such a rash deed."

"Go before me and warn them that I come," suggested Galahad.

The squire fell back amazed at such a knight, for never had he met the like.

Sir Galahad rode down to the banks of the Severn, and wicked and deep and black did the water look, with small circling eddies that argued dangerous currents. As his horse drank, he gazed up at the castle, looming near. Then he urged his nervous mount into the stream, encouraging it with soothing words so that it went forward. In spite of its look, the water was not too deep but that the horse could wade splashing, the waves lapping against its sides. They crossed safely, and then Sir Galahad halted at a little distance from the main gate. A bugle rang out, and out came seven men, armed to the teeth, a grim array. They thundered across the drawbridge!

"Defend yourself, knight," they shouted, "for now your death comes swiftly!"

"Why?" Galahad asked. "Will you all fight with me at once?"

"Yes," one of them answered; "as one."

"Come at your peril!" he replied.

So down went the seven lances. As the horsemen charged down upon him, even his stout heart might well have quailed;

but he set his lance in rest and waited. He caught the leading man so adroitly with the point that he tumbled him off his horse in a clanging heap upon the earth. The other six spears all met together on the red-cross shield and splintered into little slivers, but Sir Galahad was like a rock in the saddle, for he seemed to have a strength above that of common men.

He whirled his horse about, drew his sword, and dealt such strokes as were a marvel to see. For a short time the knights tried to withstand him, but so mighty a fighter was he that they could not prevail.

"Flee, for he is no man but a monster," they cried at last in fear. "We shall be utterly destroyed."

One of the knights flung away his sword, then urged his horse to a gallop and rode back over the drawbridge. Seeing this, the others dared stay no more, but fled into the castle, slamming and locking the great door, then galloped out again on the far side and so away over the hills. Sir Galahad was left the victor.

"That adventure is achieved," he said, and stroked the neck of his destrier. It turned its head and pressed its velvet nose against his outstretched hand, for children and animals knew Sir Galahad for a holy knight.

"Here comes an old man to speak with me," Galahad mused, and he went forward to meet him.

"Sir," quavered the old fellow excitedly, holding up a bunch of keys, "open the gates of the Castle of Maidens and the city gates and free the people who have been shut up so long!"

"Certes, that will I," said the knight. "Come, let us forward!"

No one challenged from the grim ramparts far above, no one drew in the bridge or lowered the portcullis. Eyes might be watching from the arrow slits far up the walls; Sir Galahad could not tell. It seemed as if the defeat of the seven knights who had for so long and so cruelly held the castle, was a sign that the old rule was over. The men-at-arms before the great door leaned upon their swords and said no word. With his horse stamping and neighing and tossing its head, Sir Galahad rode below the gleaming iron teeth of the portcullis. Then he dismounted and thrust the key into the lock of the main door. Strongly he pushed it open, so that it banged against the wall that surrounded the outer bailey and sounded a sonorous summons of freedom. From door to door, from keep to dungeon, he strode, unlocking and unbarring. Out poured the prisoners. Some were old and blind from being for years in the darkness, some were still young, and had been hoping each day for the freedom which had now come so suddenly gloriously. Sick and wounded, peasants and noblemen, they came out in scores, and so did the people from the city. They had been virtually prisoners too, for the seven wicked knights who had held the Castle of Maidens had been hard overlords.

"You are free now," Galahad told them. "The seven knights will not come back. Now will I go on to other adventures, for there is much to be done and I may not turn back from anything which is my work."

CHAPTER 26

THE END OF THE QUEST

FAR and wide over all the country the Knights of the Round Table were riding on the Quest of the Holy Grail. In castle court and humble cottage, in vast cathedral and village church, they sought the Grail. They questioned men and women and followed up legends that might lead them to where it was hidden; but it eluded them.

Sir Gawaine early tired of the quest and longed for the old days at Camelot again.

Weeks and months grew into years, and knight after knight dropped out of the quest. As he heard of the death of any of his knights, King Arthur created others so that the numbers at the Round Table should be complete; but never was all the old fellowship to meet again as in days gone by, with all the old great names upon the sieges.

During the quest, however, strange adventures did befall many of the knights, some of whom gave up old careless ways of living and became patterns of knighthood.

The ranks went on thinning, for this was the hardest adventure that any man had yet set out upon. Ever in the forefront of the searchers rode Sir Galahad. Sir Bors and Sir Percivale were not far behind, and their ways were coming together. Then one day they met, and great was their joy.

"Now will we go forward together," said Sir Galahad. "It is more than a year and a half since we set out. Each of us has ridden without company through wild lands, for we have come very far from Camelot, and there may be many miles to go!"

One evening, when it was drawing to dusk, the three came to a castle built upon a craggy shore falling down steeply to the sea. The waves roared about its walls on the seaward side and washed up over the slippery steps below a postern set in the outer wall. There was something wild-looking about the dark towers, over which the gulls swooped and called.

Sir Bors, Sir Percivale and Sir Galahad sat their horses at the top of a long slope, and looked down upon this strange place.

"Here we can rest for the night," said Sir Galahad, "for we have not often found lodging except below the stars this many a long day."

They rode down unchallenged into the inner courtyard, where they were met by the people of the castle, who were right glad to see knights-errant and to hear news from other parts of the land.

"You have travelled far," they said. "Your shields are not known in these parts. Stay with us and accept our cheer."

"Truly," said Sir Galahad, "for that we shall be thankful!"

He gazed about him in wonder, for he had a strange feeling about the place.

"There is an unearthly peace about me," he said to Sir Bors. "Now wit ye well, I feel that we are near the end of our search. Yet the good people of the castle tell us nothing about it."

"Perhaps we alone feel it," said Sir Percivale.

The king of that castle made them welcome and made them a gift of a mighty sword, which had been there since the days of Joseph of Aramathie. He brought to them many good and brave knights, also upon the quest of the Holy Grail. These came from other lands and had never been to Camelot or seen the Table Round. Some were from Gaul, some from Ireland, and others from distant Denmark.

When he heard of the quest the King cried: "Seek through my castle, for who shall say where you may find the Holy Grail. There are secret places in all castles, so that even I do not know all the parts of this my own home! Old legends have said oft that the Holy Grail is somewhere here or in these lands."

So he departed out of the hall and all the people of the castle with him who were not in the quest. And the three made search, and in that strange castle by the sea they found the Holy Grail. It stood upon a table of silver. They gazed upon it, and then kneeled in prayer upon the ancient stones.

That night Sir Galahad dreamed that he was bidden to take the Holy Grail to the city of Sarras, in a far country, for the people of this land were no more worthy that it should be among them, for they had abandoned old faiths and turned aside after riches and vain things. In his dream, Sir Galahad heard a voice say that only he himself, with Sir Percivale and Sir Bors, should go upon this mission. Two of them upon fulfilling their mission should die in the glory of achievement, but one of them should return to Camelot.

Next morning he and his fellows set out and took ship for Sarras, and the Holy Grail went with them, for they were its guard, determined to peril their bodies to the death to keep it safe. Many strange adventures they had, too many to be set down here, for they were imprisoned by a heathen king and risked death and shipwreck many a time. But they succeeded in their mission and brought the Holy Grail to Sarras. Yet from that day to this no man has seen it.

Sir Galahad and Sir Percivale, who were the truest knights that ever lived, died in that far country and came never more to Camelot, but Sir Bors returned, as had been foretold. He set off upon his journey some months after their deaths, back to his homeland, to the green fields and scented woodlands he had known aforetime. When he got back to the court, they all made much joy of him, for he had been gone so many years that all there had deemed him dead. They dined together, he and King

Arthur and such of the old fellows of the Round Table as had returned and all the new knights who had come to fill the empty sieges.

After meat, the King called in clerks with pens and parchments. "Sit down among my knights, worthy men," he said to them. "The knights shall tell you all the adventures which have fallen them on the quest and you shall write down as they speak."

So they all sat about and listened and marvelled, and so great was the atmosphere of excitement that no one spoke except the knight who was telling the tale at the moment. The only other sound in the hall was the scratch, scratch of the quill pens. Then were all those parchments collected and made into books and placed in great chests at Salisbury for safe keeping, that generations to come should know of the quest of the Holy Grail and tell their children and their children's children how three knights only were deemed worthy to succeed in it.

CHAPTER 27

THE QUEEN IN PERIL

AFTER he returned from the Quest of the Holy Grail, Sir Launcelot's love for Queen Guinevere began to be whispered about. To try and quieten it, he took every chance that came to ride from the court upon deeds of knight-errantry; but this displeased the Queen. She called him to her one day and asked him why he went so often away.

"For your sake as much as for the adventure," he answered. "Men speak evilly, as it is, about us, and only King Arthur still trusts us. While tongues wag it will be better for me to go on a journey. I will return when talk about us has ceased."

She heard him out stonily and then began to weep and upbraid him. "Leave the court if you think it best," she said, and she told him never to come near her again, and many other hard things she said in her sorrow and temper.

He stood before her until she had done speaking, and his heart was so heavy that he could not answer. Leaving her, he sought out his kinsman, Sir Bors, and told him that the Queen had forbidden him the court, and that he had a mind to leave Camelot for ever and go to his own home, far away.

Sir Bors shook his head. "Not so," he counselled. "Suppose that the King or the Queen should need your help at any time? It may be that Queen Guinevere said harder things than she meant, for ever have you been her brave knight. By my advice, you shall go to the hermitage at Windsor and abide what may come!"

"Gentle cousin," said Sir Launcelot, "that will I do, and tell no man where I am!"

So the great knight armed himself and saddled his horse and rode away from King Arthur's court. His countenance was sad and his heart was heavy. He rode to Windsor, where lived a hermit called Sir Brasias, who was a simple, holy man, and who made Sir Launcelot welcome.

"Where is Sir Launcelot?" they began to ask about the court, and they marvelled how he had gone so quietly that none had seen him ride away.

"He cannot really have gone," Queen Guinevere told herself in fear, and she made quiet search, but it was true; he was away, leaving no word.

She sorrowed deeply, but she dared not show it openly, but must laugh and play and be merry with the others, though she felt that her heart was breaking. Her pride helped her to hold her head high, and only when quite alone could she weep and mourn as she longed to do.

"But I will show him and them that I do not care," she said, clenching her hands. "I will make a great dinner in London for twenty-four of the knights of the Round Table." Then she made out a list of all she would invite, and she planned the dinner and what they should eat, just as any housewife would do in any century. She thought she would invite Sir Gawaine, among the others, so she must have plenty of fine fruit, for it was his habit to eat much fruit, of which he was very fond, especially apples and pears.

"Sir Gareth shall be invited too," the Queen thought. She sat by her window, and the bees buzzed in and out from the garden. "Sir Bors shall be there, and Sir Blamore de Ganis and his brother, Sir Mador de la Porte, Sir Ector de Maris, Sir Pinel le Savage, Sir Patrise, and others to the number of twenty-four."

As it happened, Sir Pinel hated Sir Gawaine, but this the Queen did not know. Sir Gawaine had helped to kill Sir Lamorak de Galis, the kinsman of Sir Pinel, and that was why he hated him so bitterly, even though he was a fellow knight of the Round Table.

When the invitations had gone out and Sir Pinel discovered that Sir Gawaine was to be there, he was tempted in his heart, for he thought that this was a golden chance to kill him without anyone knowing who was the slayer. Being cowardly at heart, he yielded to this impulse, and when they were all come to London for the feast he managed to get hold of the dish of apples that was set before Sir Gawaine's place. He poisoned the fruit, and then, arrayed in his finest robes, joined the other knights as they assembled before Queen Guinevere.

She was looking passing fair in her jewels and silken gown broidered with golden lilies. Perhaps there was a sad light in her eyes as she gazed upon the noble gathering, from which was absent the only one she really cared to see there, but her lips were smiling.

They filed into the banqueting hall, where lighted sconces glowed upon the gold and silver plate, and rich baked meats and flagons of frothy mead and rare wines awaited the guests.

Sir Patrise sat next to Sir Gawaine, and he thought how fair and red the apples looked. He ate little fruit, but now he took an apple and ate it.

"I am slain!" he groaned, for the poison was swift and deadly. With clutching hands he dragged at the cloth as he fell, bringing the dishes to the edge of the table so that many clattered to the stone floor.

"What ails Sir Patrise?" was the cry.

Sir Mador bent over his kinsman's quivering body.

"He is dead!" he said stonily, and looked at Queen Guinevere accusingly.

All the knights arose and stood dumbfounded, knowing not what to say but all of them looked at the Queen, who stood pale as snow, one hand to her lips.

Sir Gawaine was the first to speak. "This thing was meant for me!" he accused her hardly. "All men know that I love fruit, and this dish was set before me. I have been near to death and the shame is upon you, Queen Guinevere."

Her lips were trembling, but she could not get out one word, for the shock seemed to have stunned her.

Then Sir Mador crashed his fist down on the table. "This shall not end here," he promised. "My kinsman is dead—foully slain by you. I accuse you of treason against him and I will be avenged to the uttermost."

Piteously her eyes went from face to face as if expecting someone to speak for her and end this terrible scene, which she could hardly believe was really happening. She was the greatest lady in the land, the fairest jewel in King Arthur's crown.

But no one spoke, and all was silent until the stillness was broken by the sob that shook her. With her hands before her face, and weeping as if distracted, the Queen swooned in her chair. Then was such a noise and clamour that men ran for the King, who hastened in. When he saw the scene he was sore amazed and asked what was toward. Before them all, Sir Mador stood and accused the Queen of treason.

Then was King Arthur passing heavy, for, as he was King, he must be a judge in the matter, and so could not be the champion of his own loved wife, whom he was sure was innocent.

"She did not do it," he cried in a firm voice. "Never will I believe it of her. Yet must justice be done. Someone shall fight in her quarrel and save her from the stake!" In those days, the penalty for such a deed as poisoning was death by fire.

"Alas," moaned the Queen, wringing her hands, "I am innocent in this matter. Woe, woe is me!"

It was arranged at last that in the flowery meadows beside Westminster, fifteen days from then, Sir Mador should do battle in the lists against the Queen's champion, and the issue of the battle should decide the matter.

When the King and Queen were alone together he took her in his arms and kissed her lovingly.

"Where is Sir Launcelot?" he asked. "He will fight for you, as I cannot, and he will save you!"

"I do not know where he is," she said, and hid her face. "His kinsmen think that he has left the country."

"Then Sir Bors will fight for you for his sake, I doubt not," answered King Arthur comfortingly.

"Ah, if only Launcelot were here," she moaned, "he would soon end this sorrowful matter."

The King looked at her. "What ails you, sweeting, that you cannot keep so good a knight by your side?" he asked smiling gently. "But as he is away at this time, go to Sir Bors and beg him to take up this matter for you."

So she departed, sorrowing greatly, and called Sir Bors to her room. He came, and she asked him tearfully to help her.

"I cannot have ado in this case," he told her gravely, "for I was there, too, as you know. You cannot have the shame to ask it of me, for it is you who have driven away Sir Launcelot, my cousin!"

"Counsel me," she implored and kneeled to him in the depth of her woe. "I did not do it, but I am like to be burnt for it if none will defend me."

Right so King Arthur strode into the room and Sir Bors took the Queen's hands and pulled her up to her feet, and, in pity for her, he took the quarrel on himself, though it would bring foul suspicion on him and cause many of his friends to turn against him.

"I will be your champion," he promised, "unless another knight greater than I come forward."

And so it was arranged. But Sir Bors was determined that Sir Launcelot should save the Queen, for he was a mighty fighter and invincible, and he, Sir Bors, might not be able to save her.

That night he left the court by the moon's light and rode to Windsor to Sir Launcelot. By sleepy hamlet and lonely forest and moor he rode and came to the hermitage as the dawn was breaking rosy in the sky. When Sir Launcelot heard his news he was glad that he could now do something for his Queen, and he charged Sir Bors to let no one know but to carry on with the matter and hold his place up till the last minute, until he should ride in to take over the battle.

So the days slipped away, and at last came the morning when the Queen's champion should fight for her. Many of the Knights of the Round Table had been so impressed by Sir Bors's nobility that they began to believe Queen Guinevere was not to blame, after all, but some there were who still doubted.

It was a fine day; the daisies in the Westminster meadows were blowing gaily, and the birds sang carefree, heeding not the grim pile of faggots about the iron stake, nor the assembled guards, nor the chief constable and men-at-arms. The ladies of the court and the Knights of the Round Table, the King and the Queen, all walked to the place, and there the Queen was placed in the charge of the constable.

Then Sir Mador came proudly before the King and swore upon oath that he thought her guilty and that he would prove it with his body in mortal combat. Then came Sir Bors de Ganis and looked scornfully at Sir Mador. Turning to King Arthur, he cried in a loud voice: "The Queen is innocent, and I will prove it as I have promised, for either I shall fight for her this day or another greater than I, if any such appear."

Sir Mador sneered. "Fight with me or else allow that I am right!"

"Take your horse," said Sir Bors. "I will be ready!" He glanced along the road to Windsor, but no dust was raised upon it.

So the two knights went to their tents and Sir Bors armed him, for if Sir Launcelot did not come, then must he, Sir Bors, do as best he might.

Sir Mador was ready first and rode into the field, charging his horse up and down before the knights and people and crying out to the Queen's champion to come out if he dared.

Again Sir Bors looked along the road, but no dust rose, so he mounted and rode out, and right sorrowful for the Queen he was, for he knew that Sir Mador was a hardy fighter and would probably slay him, and that then the Queen would suffer a dreadful death. Then as he trotted his horse out he saw a knight come riding fully armed, as fast as his horse could travel. The sun glinted on his arms, which were strange to the company, for he was in disguise.

"Fair knight, withdraw!" cried the newcomer to Sir Bors, "for here comes a better knight than you to take up this matter for the Queen!"

Sir Bors went joyfully to the King and told him that he withdrew in place of another, and the King allowed it, but he did not know who the stranger was.

Sir Launcelot faced the crowd. "It is shame to you all of the Round Table that you believe this of your gracious Queen," he cried, and all men marvelled at him.

But Sir Mador turned scornfully to King Arthur. "Whom am I to fight?" he asked, shaking his spear.

"He is before you," said Sir Launcelot, in a terrible voice.

So they two rode to the ends of the lists, then turned and rushed together with a crash as of summer thunder. Long and hard they fought, but the issue was never once in doubt, and Sir Mador was well beaten. On the ground he yielded him to Sir Launcelot as recreant.

"Will you take back your accusation?" his opponent demanded, and so before them all Sir Mador said: "I clearly discharge my quarrel, for I see now that I was wrong." He also promised that upon Sir Patrise's tomb it should be stated truly how it had all been proved that the Queen was innocent, lest the sons and grandsons of the people there down the ages should misread and misdoubt.

"Call that good knight here," said King Arthur. "He shall drink a sop of wine with us to refresh himself, and he shall have our thanks!"

To drink the wine, Sir Launcelot unhelmed him, and all there saw who it was, and there was great joy made of him. Queen Guinevere wept tenderly to think that he should have done this for her.

Some time after, it was discovered that it was Sir Pinel had done the foul deed, but no man could come at him to slay him, for he took great fear in his heart, and arose and fled the country in the night and came never more to the Round Table.

CHAPTER 28

THE FAIR MAIDEN OF ASTOLAT

UPON an August day in London, King Arthur let it be known that there should be a great jousting at Camelot. He himself and many of the noblest in the land would be there. Heralds carried the news, and it was not long before knights were looking out their best armour and exercising their finest horses, all getting ready to ride to Camelot to take part.

The King of Northgalis, King Anguish of Ireland, the King of Northumberland, and many more, with brave array of gallant knights in their train, set their faces towards Camelot, and beside them rode dukes and earls from countries near and far.

"You will come with me?" the King asked Queen Guinevere eagerly, for ever he loved to have her near him.

"Nay," she answered. "I cannot ride so far. I will abide here in London in spite of the great heat. Ride thou to Camelot and win worship, my lord!"

King Arthur was disappointed. "Now am I sorry that you cannot come, for not for many months has there been anything like the wonderful sight that this promises to be."

"I am sorry," the Queen said.

When the King left London, he rode with all his men, and a passing rare sight it was with the colourful blazons, the fluttering pennants, and the royal banner. King Arthur made a halt at Astolat and there he stayed in the castle.

The Queen called Sir Launcelot to her when the King had gone, for she was amazed that he had not been in the forefront of the King's men. She was angry too, because she thought people would notice that he was not riding to Camelot and think that it was so that he might stay by her.

"I believe you are right," he answered dubiously. "I will ride after King Arthur tomorrow, for he is staying one or two nights in Astolat and so I shall overtake him. But you know that as it falls out I shall be against the King in the lists!"

"That is a pity," she said, "for some of the hardiest knights in the world will be on his side."

"I will take what adventure comes to me," said Launcelot.

Next day, as he had said, he took the road to Camelot. When he reached Astolat, he thought that he would spend the night there, and he also thought that he would fight in the jousts in disguise so that no man should know it was he.

Under the glooming castle walls was a fine, well-built dwelling-place. An old baron, Sir Bernard of Astolat, lived there. Sir Launcelot liked the look of the place and asked if he might spend the night there. Now, as it happened, as he stood at the outer gate with his horse's rein over his arm, asking for admission, he was in plain view from the castle gardens, where, among the flowers and along the cool mossy paths, the King was strolling with some of his knights. King Arthur leaned over the wall and watched his favourite as he was welcomed in, his horse taken care of, and the door closed upon him.

"That is an excellent thing," said the King. "I have just seen one knight arrive whom I know to be a good man at deeds-of-arms. He will do marvels at the jousts. We shall have a warm time of it!"

"Who was it?" one of the company asked curiously, but the King kept his secret, smiling.

Sir Launcelot was shown into a pleasant room, where he unarmed himself. Sir Bernard came to make his reverence to him, but he did not know him, never having met the great knight before.

"Is there anything that I can do for you?" Sir Bernard asked, gazing in genuine delight at the fine figure of the man before him.

"Fair sir, would you lend me a shield?" Launcelot asked him. "Mine is well known to all my fellows whom I shall meet at the jousts, and I fain would be unknown."

The old baron nodded. "My two boys have just been made knights, but the eldest, Sir Tirre, is hurt and cannot ride. You shall have his shield. It is well known here in Astolat, but not outside the town. Now, may I ask you if my youngest boy, Sir Lavaine, can accompany you to the jousting? I have taken a great fancy to you, sir, and feel that he will do worshipfully by your side. Tell me your name now, I pray you!"

"Hold me excused from telling my name," Sir Launcelot said. "But if I do well at Camelot I will return and tell you. I would be right glad to have your son, Sir Lavaine, at my side, and I will bear his brother's shield!"

"It shall be done," said the good old baron.

Then into the room stole a pretty maiden, her eyes upon Sir Launcelot as if all her heart dwelt in their depths. Her long plaits of hair, golden in colour as the marsh kingcup, were twisted with ropes of little pearls. She was slight as a birch sapling, and her face sweet as a May day.

"It is my daughter, Elaine," the baron laughed at her shy hero-worship. "Come here, child, and greet this brave knight."

There and then Elaine fell in love with Sir Launcelot so that she never could forget him.

"Unknown knight, wilt grant me a boon?" she asked. "Wear a favour of mine at the jousts!"

He looked down at her. "Little maiden, if I did that I should do more for you than ever I did for any gentlewoman in all the world. Never have I carried a favour for anyone."

"Carry mine," she begged, her eyes starry.

Then did he remember that he was going to be in disguise at Camelot and that the very wearing of a token would add to it, for all who knew Sir Launcelot knew that he never did so. "Very well," he said suddenly. "Show me what you have for me!"

Trembling with delight, she ran and brought him a sleeve of scarlet silk embroidered with pearls as big as peas.

He took it. "Now shall you do something for me in return."

"Yes?" she cried, overjoyed that she could offer him any service.

"Take this shield of mine and keep it for me against my return," he said, and she took it reverently into her hands.

As soon as King Arthur rode out of the great castle at Astolat, Sir Launcelot and Sir Lavaine prepared to follow him at a distance. As they neared Camelot the roads became more and more thronged with people all going the same way, so that the

dust rose like smoke; through it could be glimpsed the twinkle
and flash of arms as knights and squires, earls and kings, barons
and kings' sons, all made their way together to the jousts.

"Where shall we find lodging," Sir Launcelot wondered, "with
all this press."

"Have no fear," said Sir Lavaine. "I know a good burgess
who will take us in and no one will wot where we are."

When the day of the jousting came, the heralds blew their
trumpets for the first encounter. The King was seated on a raised
place to watch. With him was Sir Gawaine, whom he would not
permit to joust, for he knew that if Sir Launcelot was in the field
Gawaine would win no glory.

The battle began, and from the first King Arthur's Knights
did well and looked like winning, which was not surprising, as
under his banner was fighting at that time some of the greatest
names in chivalry. Then came a pause as the two sides withdrew
to have a rest and look to their arms.

"Now is our moment to join in," said Sir Launcelot, and he
fastened the scarlet sleeve upon his helm and closed the visor.
"Hide we in this leafy shaw beside the grounds and when they
come together again we will ride in."

And so they did, riding like conquerors. Down before Sir
Launcelot went Sir Brandiles, Sir Sagramore, Sir Kay, Sir
Dodinas and Sir Griflet, all with one spear. Sir Lavaine smote
down Sir Lucan and Sir Bedevere, by which time Sir Launcelot
had got himself a new spear. Now Sir Agravaine, Sir Gaheris,
Sir Mordred and Sir Meliot were unhorsed as if they had been
men of straw. Ever by Sir Launcelot's side and striving bravely
to copy his matchless style, rode Sir Lavaine, who accounted for
Sir Ozanna.

Then out came swords, and the smother, the clashing, the dust,
the squealing of excited horses and the shouts of men, were
deafening and blinding.

Upon the stand, Sir Gawaine was staring, open-mouthed.
"What knight can that be?" he said, amazed. "Never saw I such
feats of arms."

"I know who it is, but I will not say," answered the King,
enjoying his little secret.

"It looks like Sir Launcelot by the riding, but it cannot be he," went on Sir Gawaine, "for he is wearing a lady's token and that Sir Launcelot has never done!"

"Our party is losing the field because of this knight," mused King Arthur. "See how they bear back before him and his companion! Ah, here comes a band of horsemen to the rescue— Sir Bors among them!"

Three knights banded together and all came down upon Sir Launcelot and Sir Lavaine at once, hurtling at them furiously. Now indeed were the two hard-pressed. The weight of the charge was too much even for such as Sir Launcelot and he went down before them with the head of Sir Bors's spear broken off in his side.

He knew he had an almost mortal hurt, but he drew his sword, seized the bridle of a riderless horse, and leaped up to go on fighting. The three men who had attacked him and Sir Lavaine, Sir Bors, Sir Ector and Sir Lionel—who of course did not know whom it was they had unhorsed—now were in turn vanquished by him and Sir Lavaine, who was doing right worshipfully for so young a knight.

And so, in spite of his dreadful wound, Sir Launcelot fought that day with great prowess. Yet, never before in all his battles had he taken so grievous a hurt. Always when he had any of these knights, his fellows of the Round Table, at his mercy, he would not slay them but rode proudly away.

As the afternoon darkened to evening, the heralds blew their signal for the end of the fighting. By common consent, the knight with the red sleeve was the victor, but Sir Launcelot and Sir Lavaine hurried away without waiting for the prize. They knew that unless his wound was seen to speedily it was the last joust in which Sir Launcelot would ever take a part.

CHAPTER 29

THE BLACK BARGE

MEANWHILE, King Arthur was asking for the winner, the knight with the red sleeve, that he should come forward to receive his prize.

"Alas, he departed, sorely wounded, and is not like to live," one bystander told the King, who was greatly disturbed.

"These are the worst tidings ever I heard," he said seriously. "If any man find him and bring me word how he is I shall hold it as a great favour!"

"I will do that, sire," said Sir Gawaine. "He cannot have gone far, so badly wounded as he was. I will find him!"

He took a squire with him and together they combed the countryside round Camelot for several miles, but gained no word of the knight with the scarlet sleeve. In two days, King Arthur prepared to return to London with all his company and Sir Gawaine with them, but he was deeply disappointed that he had failed to trace the wounded knight.

When they reached Astolat, there was so great a company at the castle that Sir Gawaine said he would lodge at Sir Bernard's, without the wall, and so he did. The old knight and Elaine welcomed him, gave him an excellent repast, and then sat with him to chat and amuse him.

"How went the jousts at Camelot?" Sir Bernard asked, his eyes bright with interest, for all such matters were important to him.

"There were two hardy knights with white shields," he was answered. "One wore a scarlet sleeve upon his helm, and he was the finest fighter I ever saw in any field or encounter. He smote down forty Knights of the Round Table, and his fellow also did nobly!"

"Ah!" sighed Elaine happily, clasping her hands. "I am so joyous now, for he is the man unto whom I have given all my love! He is the first man I ever loved and he shall be the last."

Sir Gawaine gazed at her in sympathy. "Is he your true love?" he asked. "Then what is his name?"

"Alas, I do not know," she answered, her sweet face clouding.

"Then where did you meet him?" Sir Gawaine inquired.

Then she told him how the knight had come asking for lodging and how he had sought another shield and had borrowed her own brother's.

"And he left his own shield with me to care for," she finished. "He trusted it with me, and I have guarded it with my life!"

"May I see it?" Gawaine asked, and Sir Bernard sent for it to be brought down.

It was propped up before the knight, whose face paled. "Now is my heart heavier than it has ever been," he cried in anguish, for he recognised Sir Launcelot's arms. "And is this knight your love?"

"Yes, truly," she made answer, but her eyes misted with tears. "Would—ah, would that I were his! He smiles gently on me, but goes on his way."

"I hope that you may be happy together," said Sir Gawaine devoutly, "but I doubt it is likely. And yet, maybe, there is a hope for you, for I have known him for twenty and four years and I never knew him carry a lady's token before."

Then he told them how Launcelot was badly hurt and had disappeared. Elaine wept bitterly, but she bravely said she was going to look for him until she found him.

"Give me leave to ride and seek him," she begged Sir Bernard, and she put her soft arms round his neck, so that for love of her he had to assent.

Sir Gawaine rode to London next day very dolorous, and took the sad news to King Arthur's court.

When Sir Bors heard it and realised that it was he who had nearly killed the man he loved best in all the world he was very sorrowful, and mourned about the palace and would take no comfort. At last he saddled his horse and rode out to find his kinsman.

All this time Sir Launcelot was lying very near to death at the hermitage of a brave old knight, Sir Baudwin, who had taken him in on the day of the jousting, bound up his hurt, and tended him carefully, helped by Sir Lavaine.

Each day Sir Lavaine rode out to exercise his horse, and he came upon Elaine diligently searching the highways and byways of Camelot to find her love.

"Lavaine, Lavaine!" she cried out to him and spurred her palfrey up to him. Leaning over she hugged him. "It is good to see you. Oh, tell me before my heart breaks, how is my lord, Sir Launcelot?"

"Who told you his name?" cried her brother.

As they rode along, she told him all. They came to the hermitage, and Sir Lavaine took her straight in without warning her what to expect. When she saw her love lie there in his bed, white as the winter drifts, she could not speak for her great woe. The room spun round her and she fell in a faint at his side. Sir Lavaine helped her to recover and then he brought her weeping to Sir Launcelot again. He kissed her tenderly and chid her gently.

"Fie," he said, "if you have come to cheer me up that is not the face to wear. This little hurt I took will soon be well."

"Oh, Sir Launcelot!" she cried, trying to smile.

His brows drew together in surprise. "How know you my name?"

She told him. From that moment she nursed him tirelessly. Through the long hot days she sat by him and fanned him. By night she wrapped herself up and dozed in the great chair in his room, so that he had only to move his head in restless pain and she was awake and at his side with some cooling drink or word of cheer.

Sir Lavaine was dispatched into Camelot itself to make inquiries whether Sir Bors had arrived, for Sir Launcelot knew well that he would come as soon as Sir Gawaine had reached court with his sad tale. And so it was, and Sir Bors was found and brought to the hermitage, and there was great joy between them all.

Under the wonderful care of his faithful nurse, Sir Launcelot began to mend.

"Who is this sweet maiden who tends you so well?" asked Sir Bors, watching her as she went tripping out of the room upon some errand. "Is she the fair maiden of Astolat of whom I have heard so much?"

"It is she, and I am uneasy about her," Sir Launcelot replied. "I cannot send her away, for it would break her heart!"

"Why should you?" his cousin asked. "Can you not love her in return? It would be a lovely thing, as in some old minstrel's romance."

"No, I cannot," he was answered shortly. "Love is not to be commanded!"

It was not long before he was well again and preparing to return to London. He took his arms and his own shield again, and his thanks were warm and hearty, but this was not enough for Elaine.

"Fair Sir Launcelot," she said, with a courage she had not till now believed hers, "will you wed with me, for no other man have I ever loved or will love but you? Do not refuse!" She stood before him, pale from work and nursing, with dark rings under her eyes, and it was a sight to have melted anyone.

But he said her nay again and again, and told her he could not be forced to love, for it would be wrong to them both. He was unhappy and wished that she did not love him so sore. He told her that he would always be deeply grateful and would ever count himself her doughty knight and come to her if ever she had need of him. Someday she would meet a man who would love and wed her.

"How little you can read my heart," she thought in scorn of these last words, and she turned away and ran to her room to weep her heart out as he rode away.

Then the fair maid of Astolat began to pine for her lost happiness. Drooping like a lily in the drought, she crept about her father's house in Astolat, and never sang now at her spinning nor played her lute nor had a game of ball with the other maidens. She had no hunger for food, and each day became thinner and paler. Good old Sir Bernard tried to cheer her, and begged her to eat a morsel of food, but she shook her head. Food would not feed her when her throat was full of tears.

So while Sir Launcelot was telling of his adventures at the court in London, it so happened that he forgot all about her, and he was not to be blamed too hardly, for he did not feel for her what she felt for him.

Elaine could in no wise forget, and she became so feeble that at last the truth could not be hidden from anyone, she was dying of her love! She could not sleep at night but lay weeping softly for him in the darkness. Then she asked a last boon of her father.

"When I am dead," she said, "dress me in my finest clothes of cloth-of-gold and lay me upon a gold-draped bed in a barge and let a bargeman whom you can trust steer me down the Thames to London, so that I may pass Westminster, where is the court of King Arthur at this time, for I would once more, if I might, be close to my own love!"

With tears in his eyes, old Sir Bernard promised that it should be as she asked. In his heart of hearts perhaps he hoped that she was mistaken and that she would grow away from this lovesickness for Sir Launcelot and once more be the bright-eyed Elaine of the old days. But it was not to be.

Sir Tirre, at her request, wrote a letter for her, word for word as she dictated, and she asked that the letter might be put in her dead hand as she lay on the barge. So, peacefully as the sunset fades from the hills, did she fade away, and went as quietly from life as if she had merely fallen asleep.

In the house of mourning below the frowning grandeur of Astolat Castle all was done as she wished. She was dressed in her finest clothes and with the bed was placed upon a chariot and driven to the nearest place upon the Thames, and there was put upon a barge, which was covered in black samite. Then down upon the placid stream went the barge towards London and Sir Bernard stood on the bank to watch it go, sorrowing deeply. Past ferny woods and glowing fields of golden stubble, past copses where the bracken was already browning, flowed the river, bearing its sad burden.

At last they came in sight of the towers and turrets of distant London. It was a lovely, hazy afternoon when the barge reached Westminster, and all was very still. But the bargeman turned his craft about and rowed back, as he had been bidden, past the palace windows and so up river and beyond again to where the meadows were. Then he turned again. He continued to ply up and down with grim impatience.

As it chanced, King Arthur and Queen Guinevere came just then into a front room of the palace, and, as she talked, the Queen wandered to the window.

"What is that black barge upon the river?" she asked.

He came and looked also, then shook his head. He summoned his seneschal. "Sir Kay, what do you make of it?" he asked. "Know you anything of this matter?"

"Nay, sire, unless it is some tidings for the court," Sir Kay replied, stroking his greying beard. "I will go and find out!"

So he and three other knights went down from the palace. When the bargeman saw them coming he steered in to the bank so that they could come on board. Elaine had been a lovely lady when she was alive, but she had never looked fairer than now. Waxy-white as a lily she lay, with a gentle smile upon her pale lips.

"What do these things mean?" asked Sir Kay, but the old steersman would speak no word, but only gazed before him. So the four went back to the palace and told the King.

"I would fain see this peerless lady," said King Arthur. "Come, my lady, with me!"

He held out his hand and the Queen put hers in it, and so they two went down upon the barge.

"There is a letter in her hand," said Guinevere, gazing in pity at Elaine.

"I will take it," said the King. "Meanwhile set a watch over this barge and the good old man who steers it so that they come to no harm."

Back at the palace once more, King Arthur called a clerk to read the letter aloud before him and his assembled knights.

"Most noble knight, Sir Launcelot," ran the letter, "I was in love with you, I whom men called the fair maiden of Astolat. Pray for me, and take and bury me in the good earth as thou art a peerless knight, and so farewell, Sir Launcelot!"

"Alas, this is a sad letter," said King Arthur, and the Queen dried her eyes and sought to cheer him, but on everyone was cast a feeling of gloom. A dark shade seemed to have brushed over the sunshine of that late summer day as if the first breath of coming winter could be felt.

"Call Sir Launcelot," said the King, "and the letter shall be read to him."

So he came and heard it, and who knows what thoughts were in his heart at that moment? He turned to King Arthur. "I am no less sad than you are, sire," he said. "Alas for the death of the fair Elaine, but I was not the willing cause of it! Sir Lavaine here will tell you that. She was fair and good and I owe her my life, for only her care and nursing could have helped me back to life and strength; but she loved me out of all reason!"

The Queen was looking at him with something of reproach curling her lips. "You could have shown her some gentleness and so, in hoping, her life might have been spared," she said.

"It could not be," he answered her. "Love is not to be called up at will!"

The King looked at him and nodded. "Sooth, that is sooth," he muttered. "Sir Launcelot, to you shall it be left to see that she is interred as a princess, so that nothing lacks of richness for so fair a lady."

Sir Launcelot bowed his head in assent and so it was done. Many great knights and gentlemen hurried to Westminster at the news to take one look at the fair Elaine, and there she was buried with all the pomp and majesty of a great lady of the land.

The poor old man on the barge, his duty done, turned the barge about and rowed away up the river, and perhaps he went to Astolat some time and told old Sir Bernard all he had seen in London. By the time the flowers were all gone and the first frost crisped the grass, the name of the fair maiden of Astolat had already grown into a great legend which men speak about even to this day whenever the story of Sir Launcelot is told.

CHAPTER 30

THE QUEEN GOES MAYING

QUEEN GUINEVERE was fond of going maying in the woods and fields of Westminster, and one day in that fair month she let call her knights and told them that, on the morrow, she proposed so to do.

"Leave off your arms," she said. "We will all be clad in green, in velvet and silk, for it is the spring of the year and all hearts should be merry as birdsong!"

Ten knights agreed to go maying with the Queen, and among them was Sir Kay, Sir Sagramore, Sir Brandiles and Sir Persant of Inde. They made an early start, for she meant, at the latest, to be back with King Arthur at ten of the clock.

Now, King Bagdemagus, who was dead in the quest of the Holy Grail, had a son, Sir Meliagrance, who owned a castle some seven miles from Westminster. This knight loved Queen Guinevere and was always planning how one day he would carry her off, but never had he dared to do so, for fear of Sir Launcelot, who was so often at her side. Besides, the Queen was mostly surrounded by valiant knights and men-at-arms whenever she rode out.

When he heard about the maying ride, he smiled darkly to himself. So she would have only unarmed knights in velvet and flowers about her? And Sir Launcelot was away for the morning at another place! Let him, Sir Meliagrance, have the Queen once safely in his castle with the great doors barred, and archers on the ramparts, and he feared no rescue.

"This is my chance!" he said, and he chose twenty men-at-arms and a hundred archers, and set out.

In the meadows where the Queen's party rode, the cuckoos were calling and the robins singing blithely. High in the vault of blue the larks trilled their joy. Queen Guinevere and her knights gathered daisies with the dew still on them, and made chains and crowns very fair to see. They cut branches of green

tasselled birch and bunches of forget-me-not, primroses, celan-
dines and sweet-smelling herbs, so that they all were decked with
Nature's jewels and blazons.

Then out of a wood rode Sir Meliagrance with all his armed
men.

"We are come for to take you to my castle!" he said.

"What is this, traitor knight?" cried Queen Guinevere hotly.
"Are you not a king's son and a knight of the Round Table?
You will be shamed for ever if you do such a thing!"

"I care not for that," said Sir Meliagrance recklessly. "I have
loved you for many a year and now I will have you!"

"Take care, Sir Meliagrance," said the ten knights. "We are
unarmed, but for all that we will die defending our Queen."

"Then defend her," sneered Sir Meliagrance.

The ten knights drew their swords, which was all the defence
they had, and the knights of Sir Meliagrance rushed at them with
their spears, and so began a mighty fight. They lashed together,
and so brave and doughty were the Queen's men that, before
they sank to the earth sore wounded, they slew forty of their
opponents.

Queen Guinevere looked on her defenders, and her pity was so
great that she could not endure the sight of their suffering, so
she called out to the wicked knight: "Sir Meliagrance, leave off
fighting, false knave. I will go with you if needs must, but upon
your promise that they shall go too, so that I may see to them
and tend their wounds."

"It shall be so," she was answered.

Then they all helped up the wounded men upon the horses,
some sitting, but many laid across the saddles for weakness.
Sir Meliagrance led the way to his castle and most carefully did
he watch that all that company should go with him, for he was
still afraid of what Sir Launcelot would do if he came upon them
or heard about the matter before they should all be safely
behind walls.

But there was a little page-boy whom the Queen loved and
had been kind to, and in the turmoil she managed for a breath's
space to be at his side. She slipped a ring from her finger and
pressed it into his hand.

"Slip away, child, and go to Sir Launcelot and tell him all that has happened," she said.

So the boy waited until he could slip away, then he mounted on one of the spare horses and sped away as quietly as he might go. His beast struck a stone with his foot so that the sharp sound came to Sir Meliagrance and he turned in his saddle, and when he saw he knew that the Queen had sent for aid.

"After him, men!" he shouted. "Cut him down and spare not!"

Some of his men chased the page-boy and shot at him, but the arrows winged harmlessly away to fall pattering on the leaves.

"Lady," said the false knight wrathfully, "wit ye well that your rescue shall not come, for I will arrange it so that the knight who attempts it shall find a hotter welcome than you think."

Then he urged the party to ride quicker, and so they came into his castle. Then was the bridge pulled up into place and the portcullis slammed down, and Sir Meliagrance felt safe.

He had left an ambush of his best archers on the road to meet whoever came to help the Queen. "If it be Sir Launcelot," he charged them, "slay his horse, but refuse to fight him or have any ado with him, for he is such a hardy man that he would slay you all, and I do fear him greatly!"

Meanwhile the page-boy rode, sparing neither himself nor his horse, till he came to London. At Westminster he found Sir Launcelot and gave him the ring and the message. Then as the great knight armed him in haste, the child danced about him and prattled and told him of all the wonderful fighting of the ten knights and how valiantly they had defended their Queen.

"Now will I ride like the storm-wind to her rescue, while you, boy, seek out Sir Lavaine and tell him where I am gone and bid him to come to help me as soon as he may!" cried Sir Launcelot.

So impatient was he to get to the place that he plunged his horse into the Thames at Westminster Bridge and made it swim over to the Lambeth shore as the quickest way of getting to the spot where Sir Meliagrance had set upon the Queen's party.

Then up the bank and away through fields and woods and leafy lanes. Soon he was at the trampled, blood-soaked clearing where the ten knights had made their desperate stand. After that it was easy to follow the track because of the blood-drops that lay thickly.

He came to a long straight ride, and here Sir Meliagrance's archers sprang out of the bushes and called on him to stop.

"By whose orders?" shouted Sir Launcelot to them. "Who dares stop a knight of the Round Table from going his own way?"

"If you come on," they said stubbornly, "we will kill your horse!"

"Coward dogs," he accused them. "'Tis easy to kill a horse, but that shall not help your master, for I fear you not, even if you had been five hundred!"

At that they shot their arrows and killed his horse under him so that he had to spring out of the saddle to avoid going down in its ruin. But he could not come at the men, for all he wanted to so badly, for they were behind deep ditches which were not to be easily crossed. So he went on grimly on foot, wondering how far it was to the castle and if he should come in time. The early summer sun was hot upon his armour, so that he felt almost powerless to move, and yet he dared not cast away any of his harness. He was soon hard put to it to keep upon his way, but he held on doggedly.

Then he heard where came a rumble and the creak of wheels. A cart loaded with wood came down a path on his right.

"Let me ride in your cart," said Sir Launcelot, but one of the men said nay; he was sent to fetch wood for the castle of Sir Meliagrance and he dared not tarry, but the other man was so sorely afraid of the knight's dark looks that he hastily made a place for him and helped him up.

"Carry me up to the gates," Launcelot commanded, "for they will lower the drawbridge for you and let you in!"

Queen Guinevere was gazing from the window of the room where she had been put and she saw Sir Launcelot riding in a cart and marvelled greatly at him.

When the cart was at the gates, the bridge went up and they

drove into the outer bailey. Sir Launcelot leaped out and he shouted so that all the walls rang with the echo of his voice.

"Come out, traitor knight, and I, Sir Launcelot of the Lake, will fight with you. Come out, false knave who thought to hold your Queen in captivity. Come out and do battle!"

CHAPTER 31

THE TRAITOR KNIGHT

SIR MELIAGRANCE heard the shouting and clamour, and fear gripped him so that he shook at the knees.

"Now, woe is me; I am undone," he muttered, and in his mean heart he planned what he would do to his archers who had not been able to stop Sir Launcelot. But his mind was full of his own peril, and he ran up the stone steps and along the passages to the turret-room where he had put the Queen. "Open and let me in," he gasped, and fell on his knees, clutching at her skirts. "Mercy, mercy!" he cried. "I will surrender to you, I and all my castle, if you will save me!"

Queen Guinevere's lip curled in scorn as she looked down upon him. "What is the matter?" she asked coldly. "You must have known I should be rescued and avenged? What shall I do to save you, then, oh, most valiant and hardy of knights?" she asked, but he minded not the sneer in her tones.

"I care not what you do, only talk over Sir Launcelot, and take what cheer you like in this poor castle. All—all is yours! Hark how he shouts and calls me coward knight and bids me come out. Go to him!"

So the Queen went down the wide stairs. "Sir Launcelot," she said, "why are you so passing angry?"

He stared at her. "You ask me that? Who should be the angrier of us twain? I have only lost my favourite horse through this villain's treachery, and that is the most grievous thing to me, but I count it not, because I am in time. To you, fairest lady, he has done foul wrong, and you ought to wish his death!"

"I have forgiven him," said the Queen. "He is a poor, mean thing, not worth your lance."

Slowly, Sir Launcelot sheathed his sword. "If I had known you would have made peace with him so easily," he remarked dryly, "I need not have hurried so."

She flushed. "I did it only to save life."

"For no one else but you would I do this," he said. He pulled off his mailed gauntlet, and she took his hand and led him into the inner hall, and there she unarmed him and made him put on rich robes of velvet. Then together they went to the ten wounded knights, who had been placed on couches in her outer room so that she could help them. They made great joy when they saw him, but he was sadly troubled to behold their grievous hurts.

There arose at this moment more crying and banging at the outer gate, and, lo, there was Sir Lavaine, his horse in a lather, for he had ridden as fast as he might to the assistance of his friend.

A wonderful supper was prepared by the repentant Sir Melia-. grance, who, however, kept discreetly in the background. He was busy on a plan by which he hoped to cover up his own treason, for he had begun to suspect that the Queen and Sir Launcelot meant a good deal to each other. He thought that if he told King Arthur about it and made him jealous, then in the fuss and trouble his own treachery to the Queen would be forgotten. Yet his first task must be to get rid of Sir Launcelot. So he waited till next day before putting in an appearance and then came to Sir Launcelot as bold as could be, as if he had never shown cowardice in his life.

"You think that I have wronged you," he cried heartily and with much show of openness, "but to tell truth it was but a May Day game I played, and never did I intend it to be taken so seriously. Yet once I had begun, I might in no wise draw back! You are a right noble knight, so I will give you satisfaction and fight with you to decide the matter, if you will, and there is my hand on it!"

"I will well," answered Launcelot coldly, for he did not trust the sly-mouthed Sir Meliagrance.

"Excellent! Then will we to meat and after that shall you all return to Westminster and this day week I will meet you in the lists!"

Then was great wonder made at this offer. Some thought the knight said fair enough and spoke in all good faith, but the Queen was troubled for her champion. After they had eaten, Sir Meliagrance had the horses brought from the stables and arranged for horse-litters for the wounded knights, and all seemed as it should be.

"Sir Launcelot, would you like to see over the castle while we are waiting?" he asked. "It is a famous fortalice, and, as a man-of-arms and a veteran fighter, you will be interested in all that pertains to such matters."

His guest agreed and they went into the great hall to see the coats-of-arms, and into the outer bailey yard to see the armoury, and then up a turret staircase to look on the view.

"It is very fine, as you shall see," said Sir Meliagrance. "Step into this chamber and behold it!"

He threw open a door, and Sir Launcelot stepped within, trusting to his host's knightly word of honour that he would do no more acts of treason. The door clanged upon him. He took a stumbling step forward and found no floor beneath his feet. Then he was plunging down sixty feet through the darkness to collapse, sorely bruised and shaken, on a mass of straw; and there he lay in that inky dungeon in great pain of mind and body and in a half swoon.

Meanwhile, Sir Meliagrance hid his horse and then went back to his guests to tell them that Sir Launcelot had ridden away suddenly, so that they should go on to Westminster without him.

"He does go off quickly on all manner of knight-errantry," mused the Queen, and thought no more of it, as it was a custom of his.

They journeyed safely back to King Arthur and told him of the coming battle between the two knights.

Sir Meliagrance went about boasting of how he would conquer in the lists, for he said cunningly: "Sir Launcelot will not

appear, and so he will be for ever shamed." But when he told
King Arthur of the love between the Queen and Sir Launcelot,
he was received with scorn, and the King told him that the great
knight could answer for himself by killing him.

For a long time Sir Launcelot lay in the dungeon half dazed
by the fall he had taken. Then he began to feel better and to
wonder what would happen if he could not get out. There was
an iron door, barred across, on the outside. He shouted and
hammered on it, but could not break it down. Right so a little
window opened in the wall and a woman pushed a platter
through with some meat and a flagon of water. But she would
not speak, only shut the little window hurriedly.

She came again the next day.

"I must get out or be for ever shamed," Sir Launcelot told
her. "I must fight with Sir Meliagrance and slay him, and so
rid the world of a dark traitor."

But she would not speak, not that day nor the next. On the
eighth day, the day of the battle, Sir Launcelot was nearly out
of his mind with rage and grief. All the flower of chivalry would
be in the lists to see him win, and when he did not appear what
would they think but that he shirked the encounter? When the
woman came with his breakfast he would have none of it, but
sat upon the straw with his head in his hands, groaning aloud.

Pity came into her face to see such a fine man so distressed.
"Fair knight," she whispered, "if I risk Sir Meliagrance's anger
and let you go free, what will you give me?"

He could hardly believe he had heard aright. "You will let
me go free?" he cried, raising his head and gazing at her, hope
swelling in his heart so that his dark eyes shone.

"Aye, truly, noble knight, for it grieves me so to see you thus.
What will you give me?"

"Silks or money or jewels," he suggested. "Ask and I will
grant it!"

"They do not interest me," she said; "but give me one kiss.
A kiss from the great Sir Launcelot shall cause me to abide by
my word."

"That is a small price you ask," he smiled, and went to the
window and kissed her.

She was overjoyed and she told the story to her great-grand-children when she was an old, old woman. But now she kept her word and unbarred the iron door, and he came out into the half-light, which was to him as bright as noon after the gloom of his dungeon.

"Where is my horse?" he asked, and she brought him to the stables.

He got his arms and his spear and so rode out of the castle and set off for Westminster as fast as his horse could gallop. It was a good horse, the same one which Sir Meliagrance had picked out for him when he pretended that he meant him to go with the Queen. He thought that never had the sun been so glorious, nor the birds' song so sweet, nor the smell of the wood-lands so fair; but his heart was full of dread lest he should not be in time. He had seven long miles to cover and little time in which to do it.

As he was riding to the court, the King and Queen and all the knights and ladies were in their places. Sir Meliagrance, fully armed, sat his horse and made a great show of impatience.

"Where is Sir Launcelot?" asked King Arthur, surprised. "It is not like him to tarry thus when deeds-of-arms are to be done!"

"I hope no evil has come to him," said the Queen, and she looked at Sir Meliagrance, a sudden suspicion in her mind.

"He comes, he comes!" shouted a herald, and there came Sir Launcelot in a storm of dust, his countenance so dark with anger that men were afraid of him.

"Defend thee, traitor knight!" he shouted, and much against his will Sir Meliagrance was forced to ride and meet him. They met with a shock as of thunder and down went the traitor like a dead man.

"Get up and fight," shouted his opponent, dismounting and running to him.

"No, no, I yield me," said the recreant, for, like all bullies, his courage was soon cooled.

"Fight like a man," snarled Sir Launcelot.

"I will not rise, and you cannot kill me if I yield me," said Sir Meliagrance.

"Will you fight me if I make the odds more even?" Launcelot

asked curiously. "Look, I will bare my head!" He tossed his great plumed helm to a herald.

"That is better," thought the coward, "for if I can but slay him all my troubles are over." But aloud he said: "Uncover your left side and I will battle again with you."

"It shall be done," the other man said, and signed to the men-at-arms to help him, and they took off the armour on his left side. "Now get up and fight!"

"Stay," said Sir Meliagrance, "you are still the strongest knight in all the world and it is no worship to you to fight a poor weak knight such as I am. Bind your left arm behind your back and I will fight you."

"See to it," Sir Launcelot said, and the men bound him so and took his shield and there he stood in great peril of his life. Sir Meliagrance leaped up now thinking to have him surely.

Sir Launcelot turned his unarmed side towards him, so that he rushed forward eagerly, thinking to strike him dead. But then Sir Launcelot swung him about and drove at the other's head with such a mighty stroke that men talked of it for years after. With the clang as of a hammer upon an anvil, the blow went home, carving through steel and bone and brain so that Sir Meliagrance fell dead in the lists, his traitorous hands stilled for ever from mischief.

Then was King Arthur glad and all the court, and they made much of Sir Launcelot that day.

CHAPTER 32

THE SIEGE OF JOYOUS GARD

THE final breaking up of the fellowship of the Round Table was near, and it came about in this wise: some of the knights thought that they ought to tell King Arthur about Sir Launcelot's great love for Queen Guinevere, just as Sir Meliagrance had sought to do.

"It is shame to us and to all the court to let this thing be," they declared.

The loudest complainers among them were Sir Mordred and Sir Agravaine. In vain did Sir Gawaine, Sir Gareth and Sir Gaheris try to make them hold their peace.

"If you tell King Arthur you will break his heart," Sir Gawaine warned. "Think how brave and true Sir Launcelot has always been! If he had not rescued me from death many a time I should not be able to speak for him, and others of you here would have died but for his valour."

"I care not," Sir Mordred went on sullenly. "I shall tell the King!"

"Then will we not be of your party," said Sir Gareth, speaking for the three, and they left him then and there.

"What is all this argument?" asked King Arthur, when he saw the flushed angry faces of the knights.

So they told him of Sir Launcelot's treason to the kingdom, and the King's face whitened as if someone had stabbed him.

"It cannot be—Sir Launcelot!" he said brokenly. "Sir Launcelot, flower of knighthood!"

But they argued and brought him proof, and the King had to believe, for it was the truth. Sir Launcelot's love for the Queen, which so long had been kept secret, was dragged into the light of day.

"Alas and alas!" mourned the King in great unhappiness. "This is the saddest day of all my life, because the law says that for this sin my Queen must suffer death, and I must hold to the law. He had better keep out of my sight, for I cannot bear to see his face!"

Then he called Sir Gawaine and told him that he must be present on the morrow, when the Queen should die. Respectfully and yet firmly, Sir Gawaine refused, and he spoke right nobly in defence of Sir Launcelot.

On a cold and cheerless morning in the ancient city of Carlisle, Queen Guinevere was brought out to execution, and many knights, lords and ladies were there to see. An old man who was hiding in the press of people slipped away and went to a nearby field where was Sir Launcelot fully armed, sitting his horse and waiting for word of what was happening, for well he knew that with so many against him he dare not join the throng. He had placed the old man there to bring him news. Somehow he could not believe that the Queen would be done to death, but he realised that it might indeed happen.

"I will to the rescue!" cried Sir Launcelot, but his heart was heavy, for there seemed no knightly greatness nor honour in this work, even though the odds were so woefully against him. One man against an army of people should have won him glorious worship, but all was shame and unhappiness.

He spurred his horse and thundered down the cobbled streets of old Carlisle and came to the open place, and there began such a fight as has never been matched again by one man. It seemed that he was mad. Here and there he fought and wheeled and slashed and was gone before any man could withstand him, only to stab and slash in a new quarter. Blinded with his grief and fear for the Queen, he saw not whom he slew but cut them down, friend and foe alike. Sir Tor he killed and knew it not, and Sir Aglovale and Sir Gareth and Sir Gaheris and many more. And Sir Gawaine watched his brothers die and could help them not.

Then did Sir Launcelot cut his way to the place where the Queen was, and he lifted her up upon his horse and set her behind him.

"Take firm hold," he told her, and then he clenched his teeth as he made one last straining effort to win clear. He dashed in the spurs and his horse responded nobly and leaped forward in a desperate charge against the ranks of hostile men.

"We are through!" he cried. "You are safe, my lady! Now will we ride to my Castle of Joyous Gard and there I shall guard you from all harm."

"Yet," she replied sadly, "I shall never be happy again, Launcelot, for I can see all the future and what will come. Half the kingdom will hold with you and half with my lord, Arthur, and the country will be divided to woe and war." And she wept full sadly and would take no comfort.

Even Sir Gawaine, who till now had held by Sir Launcelot, now swore to seek him in all the length and breadth of the land to kill him, in revenge for the deaths of his brothers, Sir Gareth and Sir Gaheris.

"Call you your friends, sire," he said to the King, "and I will call mine and so shall we match him, doubt it not!"

But many great kings, knights and lords went over to Sir Launcelot's side when the deciding moment came, and the land was divided against itself.

Sir Launcelot reached Joyous Gard and rode in and put the lady down upon her feet. Then he took off his helm and cried out his orders so that the old grey walls rang again.

"Up with the drawbridge and down with the portcullis! To the walls, men-at-arms! Let none enter but my kinsmen and my friends, for now will King Arthur besiege us here. We must hold out in defence of our noble Queen! To arms!"

With creaking and clashing and the whine of ropes, the bridge rose and the portcullis came down with a mighty slam. Soon the sunlight was twinkling upon the helms of the bowmen who marched upon the outer walls and watched the rolling woods and hills. Presently, a party came riding to the castle and word was brought in haste.

"It is the blazon of Sir Bors de Ganis and he comes with his men, and it is a right worshipful muster, for there is a forest of spears and the flashing of many arms!"

"Admit them," said Launcelot, and a look of sad pleasure came into his eyes. "The old boars hold to their leader!"

Soon came another squire hurrying. "Sir," he cried, "over by the hill, riding towards this castle, is a great company bearing the arms of Sir Palomides and Sir Safere!"

"Yes, they were ever on my side, right or wrong," said Sir Launcelot. "Admit them to Joyous Gard!"

And so it went on, for company after company of brave men came to him to stand by him. Then at last no more knights came, so the castle was stored with food and furnished with arms and closed against the world, for now it was war to the death.

Again came the twinkling and flash of arms, but this time the heralds could not tell their leader that friends were on the way, for it was King Arthur's army, with Sir Gawaine and his men, for he ever rode beside the King, seeking revenge for his brothers'

deaths. Knights and archers and men-at-arms, they came moving up about the Castle of Joyous Gard, and rolled all about it
as a great sea, and so slowly settled down to wait without the
walls in a grim siege.

Pavilions were raised and guards were set so that in no wise
might anyone carry food or arms or help of any kind into the
castle. On the battlements, Sir Launcelot stood and looked down
upon that host in bitter sorrowing, but when he saw the King's
pavilion and knew that he had come against him as a foe who
for so many years had been his gracious King, then did Launcelot
weep.

His knights came to him eagerly. "Let us ride out and do
battle," they urged, "for here is worship to be gained, and many
a noble knight will die on their side and on ours before this war is
over!"

Launcelot shook his head. "No," he said. "I will not fight
against my King unless I am forced to. The Queen is safe within
these walls and we will stay here and guard her!"

So the days passed, but each day when Sir Launcelot looked
out there was the King's army still encamped about him, and he
could hear the cry of the trumpets and the clash of arms as the
knights came and went and exercised their horses.

Days grew into weeks and months but the outer gates of
Joyous Gard were fast shut against King Arthur.

"Let us ride out to battle," begged the faithful knights of the
garrison, but still they were denied.

In his heart of hearts, King Arthur was as sorry as Sir
Launcelot, and if the two brave men had been left to themselves
they would have made peace together and Queen Guinevere would
have gone safely back to her lord. But at the King's elbow was
ever Sir Gawaine, black with rage in his heart; he it was kept
the wound open and poisoned with malice. The time went on to
harvest and the fields were gold with grain and still King Arthur's
army lay encamped by Joyous Gard.

One morning in the sunlight as he watched upon the walls, Sir
Launcelot saw the King himself whom he had not seen for a long,
long time. He leaned over the stonework and hailed him from afar.

"King Arthur, leave this siege and ride away, for you will get no honour here," he cried. "You know well that I will not do battle with my noble King, the man who made me knight, unless forced by the grimmest need, and this is my promise. Ride away and raise this siege."

Sir Gawaine went to the King's side. "False recreant knight and traitor," he shouted, and he shook his mailed fist, "King Arthur will never accord with you. We will wipe your name from the scrolls of chivalry and lay your castle low!"

After many such talks, at last Launcelot had no redress but must ride out to combat, if only for the sake of the faithful men who held by him. But his heart was heavy and cold as stone, and he told his men that whatever happened the King's life must be spared. Then he and King Arthur arranged over the walls in right knightly fashion that the castle company would ride out and join battle on the morrow.

Before the sun had dried the grass, the King, fully armed at the head of his host, was waiting in the meadows before the grim old castle. A great silence was on him and on his men, so that except for the occasional stamp of impatient hoof or the ringing chink of harness, there was nothing heard.

The trumpets shrilled, and suddenly the three main gates were thrown wide and three hosts rode out, Sir Launcelot leading the middle company, with Sir Bors and Sir Lionel leading a column on either side. King Arthur gave the signal to charge, and a grim battle began, which reddened that page in the books of legends so that never more could it be white.

Like an old bear which the hounds have found sore wounded in the forest, so Sir Launcelot found himself beset by the King and all his most valiant knights, for they sought always to ring him about and slay him, but always he caused his horse to swerve aside so that he should not be forced to draw upon the King. But some of the others were not quite so careful, and it chanced that Sir Bors encountered with King Arthur and unhorsed him. Down went the King, crashing among the horses' hooves.

Sir Bors alit and drew his sword, and above the din and splinter of the battle he cried: "Now will I finish this unhappy war, by your leave, Sir Launcelot!" He raised his shining blade to strike.

"Touch him not," shouted Launcelot, as he charged up. He dismounted and held out his mailed hand to seize the King's and pull him up. "Mount this riderless horse, sire," he said, "for by me shall you have no harm whatever you do to me!"

As they stood there facing one another, the tears came into the King's eyes and he turned away quickly. "Alas that this war should ever have been," he said mournfully.

At even they withdrew, both sides, to see to their wounded, but they joined battle again next morning. Many were slain, but never could King Arthur prevail against Sir Launcelot, and· at last the Bishop of Rochester caused peace to come between them.

"If the Queen is safe from treason and execution," said Sir Launcelot, on hearing the Bishop's words of peace, "then I have done my duty. I will myself conduct Queen Guinevere back to her own true lord! Yet must I be sure, for while Sir Gawaine is by the King's side I fear foul play."

But King Arthur himself sent him assurance.

"It is well," said Sir Launcelot. "I am right glad that this bloodshed is done. Perhaps some of the old glory will return to the Round Table again. We will ride and give safe conduct to our fair Queen, all dressed in green and with branches of olives to show that it was never our will to fight with King Arthur. Make all ready! This is the best news that has come to Joyous Gard now for many a weary week!"

CHAPTER 33

THE DEATH OF KING ARTHUR

THE sunshine of earthly glory was fading from the Round Table shields for ever as events marched on. Sir Launcelot brought Queen Guinevere to King Arthur, who embraced and kissed her and forgave her, and it was a touching sight, so that many eyes were wet. But Sir Gawaine and Sir Mordred hated Sir Launcelot for what he had done, and they would not make peace.

Sir Gawaine stood up in the King's hall and pronounced judgment for the King. "Now that the Queen is back, that matter is done with, but there are other matters with which we must now deal. Before ever you came back escorting her, Sir Launcelot, the King and I had talked this matter over and decided the issue. Things can never be as once they were!" He spoke sternly and he looked with hate at the man whom once he had loved and honoured. "Therefore, Sir Launcelot, you are banished for ever from this court and from the Round Table. Leave this land and go back to your own realms in France. If it were not for the duty I bear the King, I would do battle with you, and prove your falseness upon your body, and so we should be rid of you! But as it is—go!"

Silence fell as a hush of doom. Sir Launcelot could hardly believe his ears; his punishment was much, much worse than he had expected. He looked at the sad, kingly face of the man he had wronged, at the knightly arms, the banners and blazons he had known so well. His eyes ranged over the condemning faces, and tears such as he had never known welled into his eyes and rolled down his bronzed, scarred cheeks.

"Alas!" he sighed. "Oh, most noble, Christian realm, where I have gained honour and worship, where great deeds have been done, must I depart thus in wanhope and shame? I could wish that I had never come; but so is it with the lives of all men, even as the minstrels sing, for when they are highest then comes their fall! Yes, I will depart, but know this, Sir Gawaine, if you follow me to accuse me still of treason in my own land, then will I answer you there!"

"Make no matter of that," replied Sir Gawaine. "Make sure we will follow you and bring your strongest castle in stone dust and rubble about your ears. Go from this court, Sir Launcelot, and come here never again!"

Then did that great knight turn him about and depart out of the castle, and except for Sir Gawaine, all who saw him go wept sore. Had it not been for his love of Arthur's Queen he had been peerless as Sir Galahad, and the most noble man who ever wore armour or rode to battle.

Sir Launcelot mounted his great war-horse and rode out of the court and took his way to Joyous Gard, but because of the bleak sorrow of his heart he changed his castle's name.

"No more Joyous Gard but Dolorous Gard let it be called," he said.

He sent to his kinsmen and asked them what they would do now. In loyal words they answered him all the same thing. "What you do we will do, and where you go we will follow!"

"But I am banished," he made them answer. "I must depart from this fair land I have so loved! And with no honour do I go, for what honour does a man find when he flies in banishment from a country?"

Then up spoke his own men and also many who held by him but were not kin, as Sir Palomides.

"Still will we follow," they cried. "Are we not a pack of old grey forest wolves who hold together in weal and woe?"

"We shall not be long unmolested," said their leader. "If we are wolves then will the fangs of the hunting dogs soon be at our throats! I do not trust Sir Mordred or Sir Gawaine. There will be trumpets sounding about our ears before long, and then red war."

He rode to the coast and all his company with him, a hundred knights. They had left their affairs in this country in order; all their debts were paid, all their arms and goods were with them. At Cardiff they shipped them aboard a fair craft and warped out into the open sea and so set sail for the land of France.

Sir Launcelot stood at the break of the poop and long he looked out as the greying of the dusk sank upon headland and hill till shore and sea were one misty line, though, to tell sooth, some of the mist was in his own eyes.

The rumble of preparations was already being heard in the land he had left, for King Arthur, to whom Sir Gawaine and Sir Mordred would give no peace, was assembling all his host to go overseas. Six thousand men were in that mighty army, and pity was it that the King should think to follow and punish further the man who had betrayed him. If he had let the matter rest there some happiness and peace might have been his in his old age. But it was not to be. Sir Mordred he appointed to govern England while he was away, and then over the sea he went to make war upon the lands of his one-time favourite and the castles of his loyal kinsmen. He burned and wasted the fair, smiling countryside and left grim smoking ruins in his wake.

But Sir Launcelot held proudly to his boast that King Arthur should be safe from him.

"Wait," counselled Sir Lionel, "till they are cold with the snows of winter and must blow upon their nails, and hungry so that their belts must be tightened. Then will we sally from our walled towns and set about them, all fresh, while they are weary."

King Arthur was much moved when he thought how Sir Launcelot ever tried to spare him. "Alas," he cried in sorrow, "his longsuffering makes me ashamed, for his chivalry is still as shining gold. Again and again he has advised me to depart, for no worship is to be gained in this war."

But always as the King was wavering did Sir Gawaine bid him not to turn his back upon a fight.

When Sir Launcelot was encamped within the town of Bayonne, which was one of his cities, Sir Gawaine rode out under the walls upon his charger. It was a custom of those times for two knights to meet thus from opposing forces, and out of courtesy no one joined in. So he challenged Launcelot to come out and do battle with him or be deemed coward and recreant. From such a challenge no knight could hold back, so Launcelot took upon him his arms, which he had thought never to use much more, and he called to open the gates. Out he went, plumes waving, his horse prancing and caracoling right nobly, and a brave sight it was.

"Come on and have ado with me," cried Sir Gawaine, "for this day I will bring you low!"

"Heaven defend me from ever being at your mercy, as you have often been at mine," answered Sir Launcelot sadly; "for wit ye well, then were my days soon numbered!"

Some of the glamour of olden bygone days returned, for both hosts stood to see what would become of the encounter. The walls of Bayonne were lined black with watching thousands, and all the men of King Arthur drew up in a mighty array to form as it were the boundaries of the stage on which the fight was to be.

"Hold still, every man upon peril of my displeasure," cried the King. "No one shall stir, for this issue is between these two noble and valiant knights!"

Then Sir Launcelot and Sir Gawaine made them ready, laid their spears in rest, struck in the spurs and galloped towards each other. Truly held and superbly aimed, both spears smote upon the shields dead in the centre. Gawaine's split right up to his hand-hold with the terrific shock. His horse reared, screaming its terror, then crashed to the earth, bearing its rider down. He tore himself loose from the kicking beast and swung his shield before him.

"Alight, traitor knight," he called to Launcelot, "for this battle must be to the uttermost. There is too much between us to let us hold our hands."

For over three hours they fought, and all that time, with shortened breath, the crowd watched them and groaned in sympathy between themselves at each awful stab and thrust. It was an epic fight of giants such as many there had never seen matched.

But no man, however brave and strong, could for ever withstand Launcelot, the greatest fighter of his time. Sir Gawaine went down at last with a grievous blow upon the head, from the wound of which he eventually died. Half swooning and yet spirited to the last, he gasped and struck out at Sir Launcelot with feeble thrusts as he lay.

"Fight on," he groaned. "I am not yet dead!"

But his opponent shook his head. "I will do no more than I have," he said proudly. "Never have I done such a shameful thing as to strike a wounded man. When you are upon your feet again, we can go on!"

He turned and walked wearily back into the city, and ever Sir Gawaine cried out after him that he should return and go on fighting.

While all this was going on, Sir Mordred was carrying out a plan of his own, for he forged letters as if they had come from France, and in these letters he wrote that King Arthur was slain, and that he, Sir Mordred, was thus rightful King of all England. Quickly, before any man should suspect, he carried out his plans.

His coronation was carried out in Canterbury, the ancient city whose very dust is historic.

"I will wed with thee," he told Guinevere, "for thou shalt make me a fair and noble queen. All the world is at my feet and I have all for which I always longed!"

In her heart, the Queen was shocked and overcome with grief. Only cleverness would save her now from a shame she had never dreamed would come to her. The man who had ever been her champion was out of reach for ever, and her noble lord, she believed, was dead.

"Fair sir," she begged, "if this be your will, let me ride to London, there to dwell awhile that I may buy me fitting gowns for the wedding!"

He smiled upon her. "It shall be so," he said, and he watched her make ready and ride off with her people about her down the road from Camelot to London. When she came to the grim old city, what cared she for the gauds and silks of Cheapside? To the Tower of London she went, and she furnished it to withstand a siege, and in there she shut herself with her people, and defied Sir Mordred.

Do what he would, he could in no wise get her out. Of all the noble fortalices in this brave old land, this was the strongest and proudest, and it stands to this day, dreaming by the Thames.

Word was brought to Sir Mordred that King Arthur had heard of his treachery and was returning in kingly wrath to put matters right at home.

"To Dover, to Dover!" shouted Mordred. "We will cut him down before he lands. Follow me, people of England, knights and squires and men-at-arms! When I have slain Arthur, then will I rule you wisely and well. You shall have all you want of riches and merriment!"

Many held with Mordred and armed them and followed him to the coast. He set watchers on the cliffs and assembled all his men upon the plains and on the sands.

"Do you see anything?" he cried. "Are the King's ships yet in sight?"

A day passed, and two, and yet the horizon twinkled only with the tossing, sunny waves.

"Do you see anything?" he cried on the third day.

"Sails against the sky like birds' wings," shouted the watcher above. "Here come the ships from France!"

"How many?" asked Mordred, in sudden fear.

"Carracks and ships and galleys, more than the eye can count, all coloured with banners and blazoned shields, and black with a great host of men. They come, they come!"

"Hold them back," screamed Sir Mordred. "Fight or fall here rather than allow him to land. I am King!"

As well might a buzzing fly attempt to stop the noble lion that he stings, as well might a rainstorm think to slake a forest fire. With overwhelming weight and majesty, King Arthur and his host stormed up the shore and drove the false Sir Mordred back. So fierce was the encounter that the ranks of the rebellious army broke; the men scattered and fled.

In the fighting, Sir Gawaine was struck again upon the head, and this time there was no healing of it. King Arthur held him in his arms as he died and in that fearful hour Sir Gawaine repented of his pride and of the stubborn hate that had caused so much woe.

"Pen and paper," he whispered weakly. "Let it be brought, for I must make what amends I can while yet I have the strength."

He wrote to Sir Launcelot begging for his forgiveness and asking him for the love of the old days to return and save King Arthur and fight for him as of old. He sighed once or twice and then his eyes closed for ever. He was buried in Dover Castle, by the shore of the land he had served so long.

Not many hours more now remained of that golden period in olden times when King Arthur was head of his Round Table and chivalry was at its greatest. The King knew that he must find and conquer Mordred if there was to be peace again for him.

It was on the plains of Salisbury that the final battle drew together. If it could have been put off for a little while, it might have been ended differently, for Sir Launcelot had received Sir Gawaine's letter, and was coming with all his might and speed to help the King he had for long loved and served. He and his men rode until their horses flagged beneath them, and then they took others and pressed on, and so down to the coast, there to go aboard ships for England.

"Pray that we be in time to help," said Sir Launcelot, and watched the wind as it bulged the sails.

But grim red battle was going on even then, and Sir Mordred and King Arthur came together in the thickest of the press. It was the most terrible fight in which the King had ever been, for the enemy was his own people, and it was war to the death.

A knight thrust at him to slay him, but King Arthur charged at him with his spear so that it went right through his body and out upon the other side.

"It is I, Mordred, whom you have killed," gasped the man, and he strove with one last effort to reach the King. His sword struck King Arthur upon the head and split the bone. With that final act Mordred died, but King Arthur himself was mortally wounded.

So Sir Launcelot arrived too late to save the King from death.

They took King Arthur's body up when Mordred's host had fled defeated, and Sir Lucan and Sir Bedivere carried him swooning to a little bank of grass where he could rest. The effort was too much for Sir Lucan, himself fatally injured, and he fell dead where he stood.

"Take my sword, Excalibur," said King Arthur weakly, "and throw it into yonder lake, for as it came so must it be returned."

"I will," said Sir Bedivere, in grief and pity.

He took the sword and ran through a little wood to the lakeside. As he raised it to fling it away into the moonlit water, the stones in the hilt flashed as if they were coloured eyes and he held his hand and turned the sword about to see the colours change and weave.

"It is a richly wrought hilt and a fair blade," he mused. "It were pity to throw it away. I will hide it in case some one shall at some time require it!"

So he pushed it into the long grass and went back to the King.

"Is that done?" asked Arthur faintly, but Sir Bedivere could not look him in the face.

"You have not done as I commanded!" King Arthur cried. "Go again and do my bidding."

When Sir Bedivere came again, the King searched his face.

"False knight," he cried, "woe is me that none obeys me now, but for love of a rich hilt would betray me. Go again and do my bidding, or, wounded as I am, I will slay you."

"Nay, my lord, I will obey you," said Sir Bedivere sadly, "and not for threats but for the love I bear you."

Then he took Excalibur, and he wound the gold-embroidered leather girdle about the hilt, and he stood there upon the bank and braced himself for a mighty throw. Out flashing into the moonlight swung the King's sword Excalibur. It fell in a shining arc of steel down into the dark waters, and from that day it was never seen again.

Then, at the King's command, Sir Bedivere put him upon a barge, where three queens in mourning were waiting for him. One of these was Queen Morgan le Fay, Arthur's own sister. They rowed him out over the lake, and Sir Bedivere stood upon the bank and watched them go. And in that peace did King Arthur die, and the three queens buried him, but no one has ever found his grave.

Queen Guinevere went into a nunnery at Almesbury to end her days in prayer and holy deeds, and ever her heart mourned for King Arthur, whom with all her faults she had dearly loved.

So when Sir Launcelot reached Camelot all the old order was gone for ever and the Knights of the Round Table departed; the lances were rusting in their stands and the swords lay still.

Sir Launcelot did not live many months after that day, but died and was laid to rest in his beloved castle of Joyous Gard.

So ended the golden age of chivalry with the passing of King Arthur and the Knights of the Round Table.